HOT DOG

An Onalee O'Conner Mystery

By Connie Doherty

Published in the United States of America

ISBN 978-0-9975251-1-3

I'd like to thank my critique partner Peg Herring and my readers Karen Doherty Diana Stanley, and Paula Vaughan for helping me to make this a better book.

For Camille, Jeeters, Chyna, Morgan, Morgan, Jimmy, Kelly, Molly, Boo, Curly, and all of the other dogs I have loved.

Chapter One

The police car bounced over the rough road. I put my arm out to steady Roy and looked deeply into his troubled molasses brown eyes. "Don't worry. I'll figure some way to get us out of this mess," I said *sotto voce*.

"We'll see about that," came a churlish voice from the front seat.

One Month Earlier
Flying around the curve, I stomped on the brakes to avoid crashing into the cars plugging up both lanes of the highway ahead. I rolled to a stop, relieved to see that the cars following me were also braking. No whiplash for me today. Farther down, a band of turkeys strutted to the side of the roadway. *A bunch of geese is called a gaggle. Do turkeys also group in gaggles?* Once they were safely across, we all moved on. Such is life above Latitude 45.

I motored onward towards Chez O'Conner. Since six a.m. this proud yet slightly tuckered out commercial real estate appraiser had been on the road, driving and inspecting properties near the knuckle of Michigan's thumb. Darkness was closing in as I wheeled into my driveway north of Petoskey.

"Good evening, Onalee."

"Hi, Mrs. Stirnamen. Hello, Julian." I squatted to pet my favorite neighborhood dog. *Not much beats a dog kiss at the end of a long day.*

Mrs. Stirnamen eyed my briefcase and camera. "Land o' Goshen, Onalee. Are you just getting finished with work? And, for the hundredth time, call me Maybelle."

"I am just finishing but it's so beautiful out these days I might have to play hooky tomorrow and get in a spot of kayaking. Mrs. . . . Maybelle, do you know what they call a group of turkeys?"

Turns out she didn't know either.

The following morning I upped and at'emmed at the bright and shiny hour of seven as the sun was just pulling itself above the horizon. Both sunny-boy and I were sliding into fall mode and taking longer and longer to start our days. I was still jogging most mornings but that would only last until the end of fair weather.

The mid-September morning air felt a tad crispy after our hot summer. I ran several blocks and then turned towards the beach along Little Traverse Bay. The bay, our little corner of Lake Michigan, was arrayed before me, still and milky blue. Plumes of fog were lifting and becoming one with the sky above. I would have missed this scene of splendor if I'd rolled over and slept until a more respectable hour. As always, I noted, all good things come to the diligent appraiser.

Jogging as far as the main beach, I galloped home at a blistering pace handily passing another runner, a woman who didn't look a day over seventy. Stopping and pretending to look for Petoskey stones for a while, I let her regain her ground and get a bit ahead of me. Then I re-took to my heels and chased her down. Flying past her I laughed to myself at the sheer wonder of finally, after all these years, finding a human being slower than myself. As the smug athlete (and by that I mean me, Onalee O'Conner, Woman about the World) high-stepped up the little hill to the bike path, a gaggle of geese winged overhead, honking a noisy tribute to the glorious morning.

I hurried back to my house. Today was the day I'd been waiting for, for a long,

long time. About a year ago, I dog sat for my neighbor's dog, Julian, for several months. I'd always wanted a dog, and that time with Julian had made me realize how much I was missing out by not having a canine around the house. For months I'd thought about it and talked with other dog owners as well as researching websites about the perfect dog for each person.

As someone allergic to dog dander, I wanted one who didn't shed. That requirement had eliminated many breeds and mixed breeds. Since there are a lot of great dogs who needed a home, I'd also decided that I would get my new friend from an animal rescue organization.

I'd spoken with a number of rescue groups, and a poodle rescue in Traverse City had put me on their list for a standard poodle. Months went by until yesterday when they called and said they'd gotten a big black poodle in who was only ten months old. I was driving down to meet him this morning.

I didn't know if they'd let me take him home, but I planned to be prepared, just in case. I loaded my car with a recently purchased kennel, a water dish and a big red stuffed tomato plush dog toy. I'd also bought a leash and box of dog poop bags.

It is about a ninety-minute drive to Traverse City, so I set out right after eating a muffin and coffee. The morning was still cool, with the now, bright blue of the sky was reflected in the waters of Little Traverse Bay. I drove around the curve of the lake and into Charlevoix. Then, motored over the Pine River Channel Bridge, past the city shops, condos and houses and back out on the open road.

About an hour later I pulled up in front of a small bungalow on a tree-shaded country road. Moments after I rang the doorbell I heard a lot of barking, and a woman opened the door. Appearing to be in her mid-sixties, her grayish blond hair was swept up in a ponytail. She looked trim in jeans and a denim work shirt.

"Are you Onalee?" she asked with a smile.

"Yes, and you must be Jan."

"Yup. I talked with your three character references, and everything checked out. Would you like to meet Houdini?"

"I sure would."

"Great. Then meet me behind the house and I'll go get him."

Opening the gate to the fenced yard, I slipped through. The back door of the house opened, and a great furry animal leaped out, bounded down the rear steps and ran up to me. I dropped to my haunches and held my hand in a fist for him to sniff. He sat grinning and looking at me with shining eyes as I fondled his ears. "Hi Houdini. You're a good dog." I said and I fell head over heels in love.

Jan watched us from the back porch. "He's pretty good at his basic commands. Sit, stay, come, and he'll do anything for a cookie."

"Sounds a lot like me." I looked up at Jan. "I really like him."

She smiled. "Looks like it's mutual."

I started towards the steps. Houdini got to his feet and walked beside me. Jan, watching us, said, "He has definitely chosen you. Do you want to take him home today?"

"Oh, yes!" I reached down and scratched his ears again. Could this beautiful dog really soon be mine?

We went through some paperwork. Jan told me that Houdini had been neutered and had all of his shots. "He's also just been groomed. I remembered you didn't like the show dog style so he got a puppy cut instead."

I looked at Houdini with his mass of short curls. "He looks great." After writing out a check for the requested amount that wasn't big enough to cover all the cost of his care here, I snapped on his new leash and led him out to the car. After he was safely in his kennel, I gave him the plush tomato toy and we were on our way.

The trip was uneventful and I spent a lot of it going over my list of dog names that I'd been compiling over the past year. Jan had mentioned that dogs easily accept name changes. Houdini was a decent moniker but I didn't think it fit him. Besides, part of the fun of getting a new member of the family is choosing a name. I rolled various ones around on my tongue. I kind of liked Blackberry, and he could be Berry for short. It was the tail end of the berrying season, so it was appropriate. With his black curls, he had the texture of a giant blackberry.

We pulled into my driveway about 1:00. Houdini had been given his lunch before we left, but I was hungry. I opened the kennel, attached his leash and he leaped out amid a flurry of torn red cloth and white stuffing. Whoa. That was a quick ten dollars down the drain. For his next toys I'll look into hard plastic, I thought as I picked up a round tomato eye and other pieces of bright red carcass from my drive.

We entered the house and Houdini immediately put his nose to work, exploring. I followed him around a bit, opening doors so that he could see everything. "I'll run to the store after lunch and get you some food and a dog bed, Blackberry." His head was under the couch but he wriggled back out and eyed me. "No, I don't think that's a good name either. We'll keep working on it."

I filled his bowl with cold water and then put together a peanut butter sandwich for myself. As I sat down at my kitchen table to eat, Houdini/What's-his-name turned around and around on a small throw rug beside my chair, then pawed at it and lowered himself to the floor. He laid his head on his paws and heaved a big sigh. I gazed down at him. My dog. My Pierre. My Jacques. No, both too common for a French poodle. Cachorro (pronounced Ka sho ho). I could call him Cash for short. It means dog in Portuguese. I liked it but it was too contrived, somehow.

I got up, taking the sandwich with me. My furry shadow lumbered to his feet and trotted after me. In a file beside the computer, I found my list of dog's names. I scanned the list. Hmmm, here's one I'd forgotten about, Dashiell, after Dashiell Hammett, the author of The Thin Man and The Maltese Falcon. Dashiell. The dog beside me was every bit a Dashiell. I leaned down and petted him. "How do you like your new home, Dashiell?" I murmured into his fur as he wagged his stub of a tail.

I got a little work done before it was time for Dashiell's walk. By now it had warmed up to about 70 degrees. A soft breeze drifted through the cloudless sky.

Since Labor Day, the herds of tourists had thinned out but some would stick around until after the fall color season. Bicyclists, singly and in groups still sped along the bike path so I kept Dashiell close to me on a short leash as we stepped along. A lone kayaker kept pace with us just off shore in the aqua waters of the bay.

Chapter Two

It was an hour later and my fingers were flying over my computer keyboard. I was so engrossed in the appraisal of an apartment complex that I jumped a bit as the telephone pierced the stillness of my home office.

Perhaps it would be a client desperately in need of an appraisal on their billion-dollar real estate holdings in downtown Singapore. I glanced at the phone. Not this time. "Hi Marti. How's tricks?"

We talked for a bit and she caught me up on the romance with her Petoskey sweet patootie. He had been down to Detroit to see her over the weekend. I gathered from the conversation that they were still the torrid twosome. That was good to hear. Then I launched into my latest venture with Dashiell.

"On, my Aunt Mary Beth always said, 'If you can look after a dog or a cat plus a plant for one year, then you are ready for marriage.' You could possibly commitment de-phobia-ize yourself by taking this plunge. In fact, you should just go out, willy-nilly, and buy yourself a nice ficus."

"What about a cactus. Something that can almost survive on its own?"

"Come on. Too easy. I, um, actually know quite a bit about gardening. Next time I'm up there, you and I'll go plant shopping."

"But, what good is it to become a person fully committed to commitment with no fellow committedee in the picture?" I asked Miss bossy-pants, green thumb Gonzalez.

"It's definitely over between you and Rickie Boy?"

I was afraid she'd bring him up. Rick with his limpid pools of root beer for eyes and snowcapped mountain smile. "Since he moved to L.A., it seems that he prefers the California girls to those of us of sturdy Midwestern stock."

***

The following morning it was time for Dashiell and me to jog together. We started down the street towards the county park,

Dashiell prancing along with his head held high.

We ran along the bike path stopping about every twenty feet or so for sniffs and bathroom breaks. He'd been very obedient, and I wanted to take the next step. Could I trust Dashiell off-leash? After we reached the beach, I unsnapped his lead.

Dashiell trotted along beside me for a few minutes then tore off through the sand. It was breezy this morning, and waves broke off shore. The bay was the deep blue of the early morning sky. Suddenly there was a raucous noise above the pounding surf. A large vee of Canada geese sliced through the air just north of me.

It always sounds as if they're all talking at once as they wing through the sky. Do they keep up that chatter all the way to Florida? Of course, there are probably some who tell the same stories over and over and brag about their kids and their hunting prowess to anyone who will listen. Then there are the more circumspect birds, such as I would be, who would only open their beaks when there were worthwhile matters to discuss.

Hot Dog

These sojourners had probably flown all night and were angling down towards the water to rest. Dashiell plunged into the waves as they touched down. "Dash. Any one of those big guys could take you in a fair fight. Come!" His ears must've been filled with his own barking. At any rate, he didn't seem to hear me. Meanwhile the geese demonstrated that they could out-swim a dog-paddling dog and stayed well away from him. Realizing the futility of the chase, Dashiell circled back towards shore.

Clambering out of the lake, he shot me a grin then flung himself on his back to dry off in the sand. As he writhed around, I passed him at my blistering pace. He got up and loped after me. On and on we ran then turned around at the main beach and retraced our steps. At least I did. Dashiell was zigging and zagging between the sand dunes and the shoreline.

As we drew nearer to the small inlet where we would leave the beach, I noticed a young woman walking down the hill from the bike path. Suddenly a dog shot past her, running towards us. Dashiell, knee deep in the water, leaped out and ran to meet the other canine. *Oh no. I hope they don't fight.*

I took to my heels, but there were two tails wagging as they met and sniffed each other. Then Dashiell crouched down facing the other dog in a play stance, and she followed suit. Dashiell took off, running, with the other dog in hot pursuit. By now the other human and I had met, but instead of sniffing each other, we smiled and helloed. Her name, she said, was Lacey, and the dog, a golden retriever, was Kathleen, "but everybody calls her Kitty."

The two dogs were wrestling now and growling. It was apparent that Dashiell loved playing with other dogs, and in Kitty he'd met another player. There's almost nothing more fun than watching dogs play, so Lacey and I stood and cheered them on. Eventually it was time to get back and spend some face time with my computer.

"Dashiell has given Kitty more exercise then, like, an entire beach walk with me, so we're ready to walk back as well," Lacey said. Raising her voice she called, "Here Kitty, Kitty, Kitty."

Kitty ran towards us with Dashiell at her side. They trotted together as we walked back toward the bike path. Calling them to us, we attached their leashes; there would be no dog/bike collisions on our watch. Lacey told me she nearly always walked Kitty at about this time of the morning, and said she hoped we'd meet up again.

We reached the parking lot near the trailhead, and I saw the Mustang convertible I had seen there nearly all summer. It was dark blue and probably fifteen to twenty years old. Looking closer, I thought I could see someone sleeping in it. "Hey, Lacey. Do you know anything about that car?" I nodded my head at it.

"Yeah. It's been parked here, off and on, for, like, months. The guy is homeless and sleeps in his car."

"How does he live?"

"He collects soda and beer cans and turns them in for the deposit."

"Really? He can make enough money for gas and food doing that? At ten cents a can, it would take a lot of cans for a bunch of Brussels sprouts."

"Totally. I went up and rapped on his window one time and I'm, like, 'Can I buy you a burger or something?' He said no, that he was doing fine. He has a little heater that he, like, plugs in and uses when it's cold."

"What does he do all day?"

"Most of the times I've seen him? He's, like, reading."

"I know there are homeless people around here, but I never come across them."

"Yeah, they're usually invisible, I guess. I must admit, I was, like, it's kind of scary to walk around here alone. You know, in the real early morning when it's still kind of dark, with his car here. But, then after I talked with him a few times and he seemed pretty nice, I was, like, I guess this man is okay. There's another dude I see a lot that I think is homeless too. That guy scares me." Lacey reached in her pocket and pulled out some dog treats. "Can Dashiell have a cookie?"

Both dogs dropped to their haunches and stared up at her. "Sure. Thanks."

Lacey loaded Kitty into an older silver Ford Focus as Dashiell and I continued on. A few minutes later she drove by with Kitty looking out the passenger side window at us.

Chapter Three

Several weeks flew by filled with dog-walking, new dog-owner friends and my current appraisal of a shopping center. Lacey and I met regularly now to walk Kitty and Dashiell. Almost every morning the dark blue Mustang was parked at the far end of the parking lot. Today was only September Thirtieth, but it was a very chilly morning. My thermometer registered forty-six degrees, and a cutting wind whooshed in off the lake. Both Lacey and I were wearing light winter parkas and gloves. *Could a small heater keep a car warm all night?*

"That's, like, a really hard way to live, isn't it?" Lacey said following my line of sight towards the blue car.

"Sure seems like it. Lacey, I think I saw that other homeless guy yesterday when Dashiell and I had our afternoon walk. He was scary. His eyes . . ."

She swung towards me, nodding. "Totally. They bore right into you don't they?"

"Yes. I said hello to him, but he just stared at me."

"He's never talked to me, either. He's someone I wouldn't want to meet up with on a dark night. I mean . . . he's probably harmless but he, like, gives me the creeps."

"Me too. Way to go, Dash. Nothing like placing your dog guano five feet away from the trash can."

Lacey laughed. Even though there was a rather sizable gap in our ages, I really got a kick out of my time with her. If it hadn't been for Dashiell, we would never have met. There's a lot to like about having a dog around the house.

I pulled out a plastic bag from my stash, scooped up the detritus, and tossed it in the garbage. Further on we left the partial shelter of the trees and felt the wind swooping in from the bay. Lacey and I looked at each other. It was a good day for a short walk. Sadly, that term wasn't part of Dashiell's and Kitty's vocabulary. They tore down the hill to the beach. Although we might have been able to get them back, the roiling surf pounding the shore called to me.

Hot Dog

"Awesome," Lacey said, a big grin spreading across her face.

Hearing Lacey's testament to the raw natural beauty made my own love for it swell inside me. "Sure is."

We pushed on against the wind after the two gamboling dogs and surprised ourselves by covering the distance of our usual walk. After we had made our way partway back from our turn-around, we noticed a man striding down through the sand dunes towards the beach. Just then a large dog appeared on top of the dune above him. Dashiell and Kitty were running side by side, holding opposite ends of a large stick in their mouths, and hadn't noticed our interloper yet. The man turned back to his dog and snapped a leash on him as soon as he got within arm's length.

Maybe the new dog is a fighter. It was definitely leash time. We yelled to our dogs, commanding them to come. Surprisingly, they dropped the stick and ran back to us. After popping on their leashes, we walked sedately down the beach toward the newcomers. As we drew close enough to see the man's face, Lacey yelled "Hi, Pete."

"Lacey. Hi. And how's Miss Kitty?"

"She's doing fine." Drawing closer, she added, "Pete, I'd like you to meet my friend, Onalee and her new pup, Dashiell. Onalee, this is Pete."

We said our hellos and then Lacey said, "Pete, I'm surprised you put Sydney on a leash."

"I didn't recognize you from a distance and I can't risk a dog fight. When you own a pit bull, if there's trouble, the pit will always be the one to be blamed."

Lacey leaned down and fondled Sydney's ears, "That's so unfair. He's one of the sweetest dogs around." She straightened back up.

"It's just the way it is. I even have to pay more for homeowner's insurance because of him."

I ventured closer and held my hand out to the new dog for a sniff. He seemed to accept me, so I petted him as Lacey and Pete chatted. Sydney was a beautiful dog. He was rich caramel with a white chest and white muzzle. Lean and muscular, he held himself proudly. For the second time in my life, I was falling in love at first sight. The attraction seemed to be mutual as Sydney leaned into my leg. Looking up, I said, "What a great dog, Pete."

Hot Dog

"He really likes you," he said smiling. "Look, you're making him blush." Sydney's nose and chest were pinking up.

"Oh my gosh. I didn't know dogs could do that," I said.

"Did I hear right, that you just got your dog?"

"Yes. He came from the poodle rescue."

"He seems like he is well socialized. Have you thought about getting a second dog? I'm always looking for good homes, but they're all pit bulls, pit mixes, Rottweiler's or German Shepherds."

"Pete's a guy who's, like, always up for a challenge." Lacey said grinning. "He rescues the kind of dogs a lot of people wouldn't want."

"Is that your job?"

"Oh no. I have a computer repair business. The pooches are my hobby." He leaned down. "I'm going to let Syd off his leash if it's okay with you guys. I think they'll all get along just fine."

The three dogs rolled and tumbled and chased each other up and down the beach. Meanwhile we three humans talked. Lacey and Pete were more than pleased to run into each other, or so it seemed to me. Gazes were held a lit-tle longer than was necessary. And, I'd never seen Lacey so animated. I should state, for the record, that affairs of the heart are my specialty, at least as long as I'm not directly involved.

Pete may not have been as handsome a guy as Sydney was a dog, but I placed him solidly above average. By the look of things, the smitten Lacey would consider him in the dream boat category. Standing and forming a human gale block for the two, perhaps not lovebirds, but at least intensely interested birds, I was getting really chilly. They may have noticed my hopping up and down, or maybe it was when I began arm rotations to aid the blood flow to my hands, but eventually, Lacey and Pete tore themselves away from each other, and we continued on our way.

Chapter Four

Back home I knew I should finish the shopping center report. But feeling cold into the marrow of my bones, I decided that the only reasonable course of action open to me was to cook some chili. The first pot of chili of the fall season is always a special event in the O'Conner household.

I took an inventory of supplies on hand. Since I hadn't planned this meal last night, I now had to do a speed soak of my kidney beans by boiling the water and allowing them to sit for an hour. It had been easier when I bought the canned variety, but reading the label one day, I found out they were drenched in high fructose corn syrup. All those healthy meals I had thought I was eating were loaded with calories.

Almost no one reveres sweets more than I, but I prefer to take in my sugar as it was intended: as the key ingredient in cookies, pies, ice cream and other comfort foods. Sugared kidney beans? Abominable!

Connie Doherty

Chili is a quick meal to prepare, I thought as I grabbed a couple of onions, a carrot and two stalks of celery from the fridge. Dicing the onions brought tears to my eyes. More tears than losing Rick ever had, I mused. Was I becoming jaded? Was I no longer a hopeless romantic?

I pulled out a couple of plastic baggies filled with tomatoes from the freezer and set them soaking in a basin of hot water. I like to buy tomatoes by the bushel from my favorite local farm market, boil them down a bit, and store them in the freezer for my winter dining pleasure. I sautéed the onions and celery in my big stainless steel cooking pot, reveling in the smell. Then I added the tomatoes, some water, and spices. After the beans were softened, I threw them into the pot as well. The swirling reds and greens inside the kettle were glorious. The chili would be simmering all afternoon as I worked on my appraisal.

I was knee-deep into the report when Dashiell began barking furiously. I looked out and spotted a red mid-sized car in my drive. The doorbell rang, sending Dashiell into another round of baying. My friend Ginger was on the porch. "Hi, Onalee. I was in your neighborhood so I brought you a cherry pecan bagel. They're so good, I wanted you to try them."

"Zowie. What a nice surprise. Come on in, I've got something for you, too, a bunch of beer cans from that last bonfire we had."

"Hi, Dashiell," she said as he moved within easy petting range. She gave him a brief rub down and then followed me towards the garage where the returnable cans were stored. Back in the house, she sniffed and a smile broke out. "It smells heavenly in here. What are you making?"

I turned back towards her, "Chili. Are you hungry?"

"No, I just came from the coffee shop."

"Want to take some for dinner?"

"You know me. I never pass up a free meal."

I nodded. "We foodies never do."

Handing her the sack of cans, I scurried back to the kitchen to ladle her a couple of bowls of chili, one for dinner and one for tomorrow's lunch.

"Onalee, did we drink this much beer?" Ginger asked, peering into the bag of cans and frowning. "There must be thirty-five cans in here."

"That's from a couple of the backyard soirees not just that last one. How much money is in the coat fund now?" I handed her the chili and sat down.

She sat in a chair across from me. "Funny you should ask. As of this morning, there is $180, and that's not enough. Last year we supplied eighteen kids in the area with winter jackets. Assuming we have the same number of children who need them this year, we'll need about $400."

"So. . ." She took a deep breath and made direct eye contact.

"So?"

"We need a fund raiser. Got any ideas?"

"Another yard sale?"

"Aaaghghghgh. If I decide to do that again, just shoot me."

I laughed. "I don't think I've ever been as tuckered out as I was after that last sale we had."

"Me either. There's got to be something easier than that."

We sat and thought for a while. "Hey, Ginger. Want a cup of coffee or tea?"

"No thanks, I'm fine."

Hot Dog

"Remember Mrs. Helmbickel used to tell us to put our thinking caps on?"

"Oh yeah," she said, grinning. "Our second grade teacher. I remember her."

"We both need to put those caps on, and we're bound to come up with some dandy ideas."

A few minutes later, she snapped her fingers. "I've got it. What about a cook-off of some kind?"

"Ooh, I like it. But, would we be able enter it too?"

"Hmmmn, might not look too good. She paused, "You know what, Onalee? If we decide to do this, I'll just set it up and run it. You've done enough. Then, if you want to enter, you can. You like to cook even more than I do."

We argued about it a bit, but I graciously gave in and agreed to allow Ginger to single-handedly start up and run the cook-off or bake-off. A few minutes later, with chili and beer cans in hand, she left, and I was forced to return to my lonely outpost in front of the computer.

On our afternoon walk, Dashiell and I decided to start out in the opposite direction from usual. We meandered through a neighborhood where the houses were small and many of them were occupied by renters. We walked this way occasionally, and it always amazed me to see so many dogs stuck in their owners' backyards. I was familiar with most of the people who took their dogs for walks, and none of these poor guys were in that group.

Most of the dogs were able to prowl about in the entire yard, but one poor fellow was on a leash about three feet long. It didn't matter what time I walked by this yard, the dog was tethered there. I don't think he was ever allowed inside the house. I could see him, because the house was on a corner and the sidewalk ran by the fenced-in backyard. I always called over to him, and he'd turn to look at me. He was dark brown and black and looked as if he had a lot of German shepherd in him.

Dashiell caught sight of the dog and started woofing. Brownie, as I called him, clambered to his feet and strained at the end of his short chain, barking back at Dashiell. "No," I told Dashiell and pulled him back from the fence. Brownie, scrambling around upset his water dish. The back door of the house flew open, and a man who looked to be in his fifties screamed, "You stupid idiot! Shut up!" He looked over

at us then. "Get that mutt out of here!
You're making my dog crazy."

"Sorry. We're going, but he knocked
over his water bowl. You need to get him
more water." I dragged Dashiell away.

"I don't need to do nothin!" he
yelled. "If he's stupid enough to waste his
water then I guess he'll go thirsty for a
couple of days. Might teach him a good
lesson. Now beat it before I call the
cops."

He turned around and went back inside.
I was livid. Dashiell and I continued our
walk, but our hearts were no longer in it.
I couldn't get poor Brownie's plight out of
my mind, and I resolved to sneak back the
next day to see if he had fresh water.

The following morning was sunny and
cold, but the wind had died down to a
slight breeze. The trees were still cloaked
in reds, golds and oranges, but yesterday's
gale had taken a toll. A lot of leaves had
been torn from their branches. Along the
first section of the bike path, the gnarly
limbs of the sumac were scarlet beneath the
multi-hued trees. In the parking lot, as
usual, was the small dark blue Mustang
convertible, parked at the very back of the
graveled area.

Connie Doherty

A big black Chevy pickup with tinted side and rear windows was also parked in the back of the lot, but at a distance from the convertible. I'd seen it on numerous occasions. The occupant was around for an hour or so every morning, possibly reading the paper and drinking coffee before going to work. I never saw him leave the truck, but I'd been close one day and noticed a "Don't Tread on Me" bumper sticker. I'd veered away from the unfriendly vehicle. It could have been a woman inside, but the truck smacked of testosterone.

This morning, Dashiell pranced along excitedly, hoping to see some of his friends on the beach. I think he'd forgotten about Brownie, but I hadn't. As soon as we finished our walk, I intended to see if the animal was okay.

I had a couple of extra plastic bags with me today to pick up litter along the beach. I tried to do a clean-up about once a week. Today as Dashiell chased after a soggy, sand-laden tennis ball, I zigzagged from the waters' edge to the dunes finding cups, straws, water bottles, plates and other garbage.

In a pocket between two dunes, I came upon the remains of a heck of a beach party. There were beer cans, an empty vodka bottle, a juice container and fast food carryout bags. I didn't think it had been warm enough lately for an outside party, but this may have been here for a while. I opened up my second bag to use for the twenty or so returnable cans and bottles. It was a bonanza. My hands were sticky, but my heart was light as I left the scene of my clean-up efforts. Dashiell and I continued on to the main beach then retraced our steps towards home.

When we reached the parking lot, I clicked the leash back on Dashiell and approached the little blue car. As we grew closer I saw, just as Lacey had said, the man appeared to be reading. With his short beard and wire rimmed glasses, he had a scholarly visage. He didn't look up, so I knocked lightly on the driver's side window. He opened it and looked at me questioningly. "Hi. Um. . . I found a bunch of beer cans on the beach. Can you use them?"

He gave me a half smile. "Sure. Thanks." He saw me hesitate, unsure what he wanted me to do with them. "Just set them down. I'll get them later."

I smiled back. "Okay. Bye." Dash and I continued on our way to our comfortable, warm home.

* * *

About an hour later I drove to Brownie's house. I had filled up a jug with water in case he needed it. I parked my car on the street across from the house and made my way over to the fenced-in backyard. I saw Brownie lying on his stomach, head on his outstretched paws, eyeing me. Beside him lay his still over-turned plastic bowl.

I studied the house for any signs of movement but all was quiet. Dropping the water container as gently as possible into the yard, I hoisted myself over the fence.

Brownie got to his feet, tail wagging. Not knowing him except from a distance, I crouched down and approached slowly. I stayed just outside the range of his leash and reached my fisted hand toward him to sniff. He made no move to bite, so I slowly reached in and petted his neck. "Good boy, Brownie. You're a good, good dog. He'd probably never heard those words before. Righting his dish, I poured clean water into it.

"Hey! What the hell do you think you're doing? Get away from my dog!"

Chapter Five

I hadn't seen Brownie's owner come to the back door. I stood up and faced him. Not wanting to make things worse for Brownie with this ogre, I tried placating him. "I'm sorry sir. He's a really sweet dog, and I noticed he needed water. I was sure you wouldn't mind me helping him out."

"I do mind." He started coming down the stairs towards me. "You're trespassing. Get off my property. Now!"

"I'm going. I'm sorry." I backed away from him. He strode to the side of his back porch as I turned and quickly retraced my steps to the fence. I had gotten one leg over the top of it when I felt icy water drilling me from behind. He continued to spray as I finished clambering over. I was shaking from cold as I looked back at the jerk, smirking at me. I was out of range now so he turned the hose on poor Brownie. His yelps were ringing in my ears as I threw myself into the car.

When I got home I again called the animal control officer to report the abuse of poor Brownie. Then I filled a bathtub full of hot water and soaked the chill from my bones.

Later that day, I drove slowly by Brownie's house. He was still in his yard. I wondered if animal control had checked on him.

* * *

On our morning walk the next day I was recounting my tale to Lacey when Pete appeared with his dog, Sydney.

"Onalee, that's terrible. You've got to tell Pete about it."

I felt uncomfortable, not knowing Pete very well. I didn't think I came off looking all that great, sneaking into someone's yard and getting hosed down for my trouble.

Lacey sensed my reticence. "Come on, Onalee. Remember, I told you that Pete, like, helps dogs in trouble."

"How do you do that?" I asked.

"I take in dogs that nobody wants and find them good homes." He reached down and unsnapped Sydney's leash. "So, what's going on?" He asked, looking at me as we resumed our walk down the beach.

I filled him in on the sordid tale of poor Brownie. "What do you think?"

Hot Dog

"It's terrible," Pete said, shaking his head. "Poor dog. Good for you though, for being willing to stick your neck out."

"I guess. But, what good did it do? Brownie may be worse off now than ever."

"Yeah, I know," he said softly. "What kind of dog is Brownie?"

"I'm pretty sure he's a mix. It looks like he has a lot of German shepherd in him."

"Oh, like, totally up your alley, Pete," Lacey said.

"What do you mean? I don't think that creep will give him up," I said. We had all stopped as I scooped up some dog leavings.

Pete, facing me, shook his head again. "A lot of times they won't. Though why anyone wants to have a dog that is kept tied out in the backyard, I'll never know."

"Is there anything you can do, Pete?" Lacey asked. We were once again ambling along behind our furry charges.

Pete turned away. "I don't know, Lace. I'll see."

I looked back and forth between the two of them. What was I missing? "What do you mean? What could you do, Pete?"

Lacey turned to me, "Pete, like, knows some people,"

"Lacey, drop it." Pete commanded and then strode away from us.

Lacey shrugged and we hurried to catch up with him. The rest of our walk was uneventful. Idle chitchat filled the void from all that was left unsaid.

As usual, Pete left us before we reached the bike path, and Lacey and I continued on alone. I pumped her for information, but she remained noncommittal. "I don't, like, really know anything?" She mumbled, studying the trees instead of making eye contact. I finally had to let it go.

As we left the beach, we talked about the upcoming cook-off. She was planning on entering as well. The only problem was, she didn't know how to cook. We rounded a turn in the path and were suddenly face to face with the haunted looking homeless guy. We both blurted out hellos before we could catch ourselves. He stared and took a wide path around us and the two leashed dogs. As we watched, he cut down into the thicket near the creek.

"He goes that way a lot and stays there for, like, a long time." Lacey said.

"Wonder what he does?"

Hot Dog

"Who knows? But I'm, like, it creeps me out that he's in those woods all of the time? I've seen him standing behind a tree. I don't know if he's watching me or someone else. Maybe he's just trying to stay out of everyone's sight?"

Later that day and the next, I drove by Brownie's house. I hoped the neighbors weren't getting nervous about my frequent forays down their street. Both times I saw Brownie still tethered on his very short leash. It didn't seem as though animal control was going to perform much of an intervention for the poor dog.

Chapter Six

I had just walked in the door with Dashiell when Ginger bounced up. "I've got news about the cook-off. Ladies . . . and gentlemen, start your ovens." She chuckled.

"Lay it on me, Sister." I said unzipping my jacket.

Ginger took her coat off, and we both sat down in my living room. "They're willing to let us hold it in the Starr School gym. And get this."

"Yeah?"

"They'll let us have the gym for free."

"Great," I said and cocked my head. "But wouldn't they normally? I mean you're doing this to provide coats for some of their kids."

She nodded. "So you'd think. But I had to talk a blue streak to get them to see it that way."

I smiled, thinking of Ginger, the ever so persuasive one. "Have you decided yet what we're going to be cooking off?"

Hot Dog

She leaned in towards me, "Here's what I know so far. It'll be on Saturday, November Seventh at 11:00 in the morning and we're going to charge a three dollar entry fee for each dish entered. Then, people can come and try all of the entries for a donation. I'll supply beverages. Someone can have a delicious lunch for whatever they can pay and support a good cause. We'll rake in money on both ends.

"I like it. But what are the categories going to be?"

"I was kind of thinking soups and cookies."

"Hmmm. I'll have to get busy if I want to enter two dishes."

"Got any ideas yet?"

"None. This will force me to re-open the O'Conner test kitchen. You know, I think you could raise the prices for the entries, and charge $5.00 or $6.00 for the lunches and still get a lot of people."

"Maybe, but I want it to be affordable for everyone. We should be able to make enough money." She jumped up. "Anyway, you've got to get back to work, but I just had to tell you the big news."

I looked up at her, "Hey, Ging, will there be a vegetarian and a meat category for the soup?"

"Ooh, I hadn't thought of that. I guess there had better be, eh?"

"Absolutely. Do they have to be original recipes?"

"No, that would be too hard. But they can be."

Ginger left and I went back to my computer to continue typing my latest project, a lighthouse on Lake Huron. It's one of O'Conner's Axioms of Appraising that waterfront properties usually get appraised during the coldest, snowiest days of winter. I was lucky this time that it was only autumn. It was an interesting job, and although I'd have to keep the location confidential, by appraising an unusual property like a lighthouse, I'd have great bragging rights at appraiser meetings for years to come.

The bake-off kept popping up in my mind. *What should I make?* Honestly, I had thought she'd have a chili cook-off like most organizations have. Leave it to Ginger to change things up a bit.

There was one flavor sensation for soup that I had been thinking of for a while. It might be great. Then again, it could be hideous. I'd have to make up a very small batch and see. Now for cookies. They would probably have to be some sort of peanut butter creation. I was envisioning a bar cookie. Yes, an over-the-top bar cookie. Now, back to that lighthouse. Although, it is almost dinnertime. Maybe it's time to run my first test pot of soup.

Three hours later
Thankfully, I had made a very small batch of the soup. It seems that no matter how I try to pair two of my favorites, peanut butter and yogurt, it turns out just plain dreadful. I worked on the report again for a while. In some cases, lighthouses along the Great Lakes have been sold to private individuals. To my surprise, the sales showed no premium was paid by the buyers for their historical value. They were bought and sold as if they were typical waterfront homes.

The property I was appraising had been remodeled for use as a residence and lived in for many years. It was a house, except it had walls that were two feet thick, and a circular stairway inside a tower up to the room where the light used to be. The lighthouse was perched at the very edge of a rocky cliff on a promontory jutting out into the lake. Not a good location for boating and swimming, but the panoramas were spectacular. Far to the northwest, I'd seen the Mackinac Bridge arching over the lake.

The following morning, Dashiell and I ran into a cute dog named Riley, and Susan, his owner. We'd walked with them a few times in the past several weeks. Riley was a Tibetan terrier that Susan had adopted from the Humane Society. He and Dashiell romped down the beach together as Susan and I followed along behind them.

"Onalee, guess what this scofflaw did last night."

"Who? Sweet Riley?"

"You mean wily Riley. He was somehow able to jump up and grab a steak that I'd put out on my counter to defrost."

Riley, possibly reliving his exploit, pranced along, holding his tail up high and curled over his back.

"He's not that big. How could he . . ."

"Jump straight up in the air and grab a steak off a high counter? You've got me. I keep telling him there are lots of reasons why he's been sent to the pound . . . over and over. If he doesn't start watching his p's and q's, he might just find himself back there again."

"Yeah, right." Susan was one of the biggest animal lovers I knew. Her Tibetan Terror, as she called him, had been a trial, though. He had eaten a hole in her wood blinds one night during a thunder storm and had ruined screens throughout her house on another occasion.

As we traipsed along she filled me in on her latest problem. Last Sunday, Susan and Riley sat down to watch television together. After an hour or so, Susan got up to make dinner and turned the TV off. Riley barked until she turned it back on. She chuckled and let him watch for the rest of the night. But, now he wanted to watch the tube every day.

"Does he have a favorite channel?"

"That's the first question that everyone asks. And yes, the Animal Planet," she said grimly.

"Can't you just turn the set off?"

"That's everybody's second question." She nodded and continued, "So you'd think. But his barking drives me crazy, so I turn it back on for him."

Connie Doherty

We were nearing the end of our walk. The little blue Mustang with the homeless man in it was pulling out of the parking lot as we approached. Susan watched it drive off. "I wonder where he goes."

"I've heard that he drives all around to places where he can find returnable bottles."

"And that's how he lives?"

"That's what Lacey says."

The dark Chevy pickup with Mr. Don't-Tread-on-Me was hunkered down in its usual spot at the other end of the parking lot.

* * *

That afternoon, I worked on my lighthouse appraisal for a while, doing more research on the Internet. After a couple of hours, I decided to give myself a break and drop by my neighborhood grocery store to pick up a few items for my larder. I grabbed my medium-weight fleece jacket, two poop bags, one eager dog and headed out the door.

The shopping center was north of my house, and I decided to drive there via the circle-around southern route, which would take me past Brownie's house. I didn't know what I could do for the poor boy, but I wanted to continue monitoring his situation. I had called animal control again and left a message, but no one called me back.

As I crossed the road that skirted his block, I saw the dancing lights of emergency vehicles ahead of me. I continued down the street and noticed that they were clustered near Brownie's house. Oh no. I parked the car a half block away and eased out from behind the wheel. As I walked closer, I could see police officers walking around in Brownie's backyard.

Chapter Seven

People clustered on the sidewalk near the fence. I walked over to them. "What's happened?" I asked a gray haired man watching the proceedings.

"I believe they've found someone dead in there." He pointed with his chin at Brownie's house.

"Really? Do they know who it is? Is the dog okay?"

He frowned at me. "That mutt that's always back there?"

"I guess so. He's a brown and black dog. Really friendly."

People around me had been talking in low tones but a hush fell over everyone and their heads swiveled towards the house. As we watched, two men carried a gurney down the front steps. A sheet entirely covered the person under it, the universal sign of death. The body was placed into the waiting ambulance and it motored quietly away.

I spotted my friend Susan, Riley's owner, and threaded my way over to her. "Do you know who that was?" I asked her.

Hot Dog

She turned to me, "There has only been one person living in that house for a long time so I imagine it was him, Gerald Pembower."

"The owner of the house? What was he like?"

"Awful. Bad neighbor. Terrible husband. Rotten dog owner. If it is him, I and the whole neighborhood will rejoice."

Was this my friend, mild-mannered Susan, talking? She must've seen a shocked look on my face because she said, "I know they say that you shouldn't speak ill of the dead, but if ever there was a time to break that rule, it's now."

"I had a bit of trouble with him myself." I told her about my escapade. "Do you know if Brownie is all right? I don't see him anywhere."

"I haven't either. Maybe animal control has him. Anyway, I'm glad you tried to help Roy out. That's Brownie's actual name. He and I fought over Roy more than once. But, he also blamed me for calling the police on him late at night when he was drunk and playing his country music at ear-shattering decibels. A couple of times it was me, but I wasn't the only one who called.

"Did he have fights with the other neighbors?"

"Oh yeah. Dick, who lives right next to him, couldn't stand him. He'd caught Pembower threatening his kids."

"Really?"

"Yup. His boy. He was about six or seven at the time, and he snuck into Pembower's yard to retrieve a ball. As you well know, he doesn't like anyone on his property. He grabbed the kid and was cussing a blue streak at him when Dick saw them. Then the two of them got into it." She sighed, "I tell you, he's been the talk of the neighborhood for years."

The crowd was beginning to dissipate, and I suddenly remembered that Dashiell was probably getting anxious for his afternoon sojourn. I bid Susan good-bye and hoofed it back to the O'Conner-Mobile. Where in the world was Brownie/Roy?

Chapter Eight

Dashiell and I decided that a walk along the beach was just the ticket to calm us down, so we drove back to the O'Conner manse to begin at our routine starting point. I also hoped to run into Lacey so that we could discuss this latest development. Unfortunately, I figured she would be ensconced in her job at a doctor's office. Of course, I could call her, assuming it was okay to interrupt her work and if I could remember which doctor she worked for.

I couldn't even wait and call her after work since I knew her only as Lacey the dog-walker. One of the odd things about dog people, I'd noticed, is that they always remember the dogs' names but not those of their owners. And so it was that I distinctly remembered an occasion when Lacey had introduced herself in my presence, but I could only recall her first name. And, of course canine Kathleen Susanne, AKA Kitty or Kitty Sue, Dashiell's number one girlfriend.

Connie Doherty

As Dash and I ambled through the neighborhood, I kept my eye out for Roy. *Where is that dog and is he okay*? We hadn't gone very far along the walkway when Dashiell veered off to find an outdoor toilet. He'd chosen well; there was no nearby poison ivy to threaten his clean-up crew.

We walked on and came to the beach path. From this vantage point it is possible to see around the curve of our bay and for about a mile along the shore. The area was deserted. Or, so it looked. Who knew how many large angry men carrying hatchets were lurking in the wooded areas ringing the lake. This time the D-Dog and I would stay on the sidewalk.

We traipsed along for about a mile before turning around and retracing our steps. We didn't spot Roy. In fact, nobody crossed our path on this chilly autumn day. As we got within range of the parking area near the beach, a patrol car pulled in. It motored slowly over the gravel lot and then drew to a stop.

A policeman climbed out of the car and went over to where the scary-looking homeless guy sat on a bench. The officer put one foot on the seat next to the guy and leaned towards him. While the cop was talking with him, the homeless man stared at the ground. I realized I had slowed down. I could take Dashiell to the other side of the parking lot and give the two some privacy. Or . . . Hmmm. . . What would Marti do? I forged ahead straight towards the two men.

"You're going to have to come down to the station." The officer stepped back, and the fellow got to his feet.

When they reached the patrol car, the policeman frisked the guy and then put him in the rear seat. *I wonder what that is all about.*

Dash and I proceeded along the bike path beneath a stand of birch trees, golden leaves fluttering in the breeze. We then meandered through a group of crimson sumac shrubs to reach the road. Other than a squawking crow, we saw no one else and were soon climbing the front porch steps of chez O'Conner.

***

"Marti. We have another body."

"What? Onalee. What happened? Give me details. Were you the one who found it this time?"

"No. But I did kind of know the guy. He was that nasty turnip who sprayed me with a hose while I was trying to help his dog."

"Ohhh, I remember you telling me about that pond scum." She paused. "At least Frank has an iron-clad alibi this time."

Main squeeze Frank had been a strong suspect in a murder and arson investigation that I had headed up the previous year.

Headed up might be a bit of an exaggeration, but I did almost single-handedly snare the perp. My valiancy had netted me very little in the way of much deserved accolades, and I strongly doubted that I would lend a hand to the police in this instance. Just the thought of that surly Detective Costas was almost enough to make this vegetarian/pacifist rip baby lettuce apart with my bare hands. Now what was Marti nattering on about?

". . . you solve another case you could probably quit appraising and become a private eye."

"What? I'm staying far away from this investigation."

"Oh, On," she sighed. "Listen. This fell right into your lap. Think of the adventure. You can't fribble away a great opportunity like this."

"Your goading last time almost got me killed, Missy."

"Who are the suspects so far?"

"We must have a bad connection because you don't seem to hear me. Anyway, I've got a thousand things to do, not one of them related to this crime. Oh, and I have another call coming in. Gotta go. Bye-yee"

"On. On. . . "

Sometimes there is no sweeter sound than a dial tone.

Chapter Nine

"So they took him in for questioning. I wonder why. Just because he's homeless he's, like, a suspicious character? That doesn't seem right." Dashiell, Kitty, Lacey and I were on the beach near the water's edge. A sharp wind pushed against us, coming from the northwest.

"No, but remember we were scared of him. He's creepy. Then again, I wonder what connection he'd have to Pembower, the dead guy."

"I don't know for sure, but the area that we usually see the homeless person in isn't that far from Pembower's house. About a mile, is all." Lacey said then turned her head away from me and mumbled something.

"What did you say?"

"Nothing."

"Yes, you did. It sounded like you said, 'I hope it was him.'"

She bent to pick up a stick to throw for Kitty. "What I meant was, it would be good if they caught the murderer. We could all, like, rest easy." She heaved the stick. "As it is now, I think, like, twice before I take Kitty for her evening walk since it's already dark at 7:30 this time of year."

"I know what you mean, but Dashiell and Kitty are both big enough that they're some protection." Dashiell had beaten Kitty to the stick. He pounced on it and took off running with Kitty on his heels. "Go Dash," I yelled against the wind.

Kitty caught up and yanked the stick out of Dashiell's mouth. She spun around and galloped back to Lacey, dropped the prize at her feet, and looked up at her with shining eyes. "Yes!" Lacey shouted, pumping her fist in the air. "Way to go, Kitty. Let's hear it for girl-power." She laughed as she picked up the stick and hurled it again, before chasing after her.

Ah, to be twenty-five again, I thought watching the two of them cavort with seemingly boundless energy.

"Speaking of dogs for protection, have you seen Pete lately?" I asked when she returned.

"No, I haven't, but I'm sure he's okay."

That was an odd comment. I turned to study her face for clues, but it was closed. "Why wouldn't he be? I just wondered what he was up to these days," and, of course, if the two of them were making any headway in the luv department. They'd make such a cute couple.

"Like I said, he's fine."

After many more stick tossings and retrievals, we wended our way back to the wooded area near the stream. I stared into the shadows as Lacey did the same. If the homeless person was there, we didn't see him. "I guess he might still be in the hoosegow," I said.

She turned and stared at me. "The hoose-what?"

"The hoosegow. The jail."

"Oh. Yeah, I bet he did do it." She looked away from me.

A few minutes later, they sped off in their car, leaving Dash and me to our own devices. For him, that meant a lot of sniffing and leg lifting. For me it amounted to pondering Lacey's odd behavior and also how the scary homeless guy could be involved in the murder. Meanwhile, our other homeless man sat in his little car at the far end of the parking lot, probably reading a book. I wondered if he'd seen anything. He was around all of the time, but I'd never known of him and the scary man to interact.

Tomorrow, I would get Lacey to go over and talk to him.

* * *

The rest of the day was spent pecking away at my computer keyboard and making phone calls, gathering additional information for my appraisal. A few of the sales I found were of lighthouses that were located out in the water, miles from the main shore. What a remote place to live. *I think I'd go a little stir crazy living like that. I might even go so far as to keep a tidy, dust-free house.* The phone interrupted my thoughts of this improbable vision. It was a doctor's office, calling. *Must be a wrong number. Although, sometimes an appraisal is just what the doctor ordered.*

"Hello, this is Onalee O'Conner."

"Onalee." The voice was low and insistent. "You've got to help me. I'm at work so I can't talk long."

"Lacey?"

"Oh, sorry. Yes, it's me. Onalee, it's Pete. They think he killed Pembower."

All of those slightly askew comments Lacey had made earlier started to make more sense, but still it was odd. "Why would they think that?"

"Because of the dog," she said, like I should have connected the dots. "But Pete swears he didn't take him."

"What? You've got to fill in the blanks for me, Lacey."

"Yes, Doctor. Right away . . . Onalee, I've, like, got to go. I'll call you back if I get a chance."

She was gone. I just looked at the phone for a few seconds while I thought about what she had said and didn't say. *Now that she'd dropped this bomb, I was supposed to return to my appraisal, while I calmly waited for more information? Ha!*

I had managed to soldier on, mainly due to an impending deadline. About an hour later, once more the ringing phone brought me back from the rocky shoals of my lighthouse report. It was that doctor's office again. "Hello, this is O'Conner Appraisal Services."

"It's me again, she whispered. "So, like I was telling you, they hauled Pete into the station for questioning."

"Let me see if I have this straight. You think possibly Pete stole Roy the dog from Pembower's yard?"

Hot Dog

"Um . . . there may be a few things I haven't totally told you? Pete knows some people who know some people. At least that's the way he talks about it."

"That seems logical so far."

"Onalee, they steal dogs. Remember that day on the beach when I started to ask if he could do anything about Brownie?"

"I do remember. I also remember Pete hushing you up."

"Yeah, well. . . of course what they do isn't totally recognized in some circles as legal."

"I've heard of vigilante types who swoop in and take a dog who is being mistreated. Is that what Pete does?"

"Like I said, Pete just—"

"I know," I broke in, getting slightly exasperated. "He knows some people who know some people. He himself is as innocent as a newly hatched chickadee. So, why is he in jail?"

"It seems that the police heard about this dog protection program? And that Pete isn't, like, a stranger to it?"

"Ohhh," as if that wasn't a foregone conclusion. "So the police think the person or persons who took Roy may have also committed a bit of murder."

"Yes and I . . . I know Pete and he couldn't hurt a . . . well I guess he has hurt fleas when they've been bugging his dogs, but you know what I mean."

"Do you think he or he and his friends stole Roy?"

"Maybe." And still she left out more than she put in.

"That's too bad for Pete, but I'm sure he'll be fine. I'm kind of in a deadline situation here on this appraisal and I'm going to have to let you go. I'll probably see you tomorrow on the beach."

"Onalee, wait. You've got, like, experience with this. You've got to help him."

"Lacey." I felt a small smile play on my lips as I allowed myself to bask, just for a moment, in the glow of her recognition of my exploits past. "It was just the one time that I got involved with a murder investigation. I'm hardly an expert."

"But I don't, like, know where to begin to try to clear his name. Please?"

"Let's not go hog-wild here. Just because they're questioning him doesn't mean they'll lock him up. Let's give it a day or so."

Hot Dog

"Okay," she said, crestfallen.

We said our good-byes and I was once again ensconced in the Land of the Never-Ending Appraisal. After a few small breaks and some large teeth-nashings, I finished the job, and emailed it to the bank.

As soon as the report was done, I ran out and grabbed the newspaper from its delivery box. A murder is rare in Northern Michigan, and Mr. Pembower's death had made the front page, above the fold. Reading the article, I learned that the victim was shot in his kitchen by his own hand gun and that the police were continuing their investigation.

I laid the newspaper aside. It was about 8:30, and time for Dashiell's last excursion before bedtime. As I followed behind the big dog, I wondered if tousle-haired Pete was feasting on the sweet taste of freedom yet or if he was languishing in the county jail.

By mutual agreement, Poodle-Boy and I kept our evening walk brief. It was a star-studded night, and I quickly spotted the Little Dipper and the North Star. Living in a small city above the 45th parallel, we're often treated to beautiful night skies. I had lived near Detroit, Michigan, where on clear nights there were only a handful of visible stars. I never again want to stick myself where the stars don't shine.

Chapter Ten

"They let Pete go but, I think he's, like, their top suspect." Lacey told me the next morning as we strolled along just above the high water line of the shore. The lake was a shimmery pewter this morning under a sky full of low, dark clouds. A slight breeze stirred the tops of the trees. Dashiell and gal-pal Kitty left us to explore behind the dunes. Since that could mean any number of different things, most of them trouble, we both veered off our set course to hunt them down.

"You talked with him?" I asked.

"Yes, and I think he wants to speak to you about it."

"Really. I wonder why." I said, allowing a bit of suspicion to color my voice.

Lacey, glancing over at me as we walked, suddenly stumbled over an exposed root and went down into the beach grass and sand.

"Are you okay?" I asked, stooping down to her.

Connie Doherty

"Yeah. I guess I'd better watch where
I'm going after this, though." She
scrambled to her feet and we continued over
the dune and into a camping area, deserted
now until next spring. We called for our
wayward dogs that we spotted, dancing near
a tree a few hundred yards away.

We both took to our heels and galloped
towards them. There, with his back against
a maple, was a large porcupine. The two
dogs were staying several yards away from
him. Dashiell saw me, and gathering his
courage, decided to move in for a closer
inspection. "Nooooo!" I screamed at him.
Startled, both he and Kitty jumped back. We
rushed over to them, attached their
leashes, and pulled them away from the poor
cornered porky.

We kept them leashed until we were
back on the beach. "That was a close one."

"Oh, totally," Lacey said
breathlessly. "Now where were we? Oh yes.
Pete. He doesn't say it but I know he's
really scared. We've got to help him."

"Lacey, take it from me, nosing around
in a murder investigation isn't as much fun
as it sounds."

She stopped and turned towards me,
frowning. "Seriously? I don't think it

sounds like any fun at all. But I have always thought that standing by your friends is, like, the right thing to do. I guess I took you to be someone who would agree with that."

"I don't even know Pete that well. He seems to be involved with some activities that are possibly illegal, but neither you nor he has ever confided in me about what they are. Now you want me to go out on a limb for him when for all I know he's Pembower's killer? I don't think so."

***

Around five o'clock I decided to take a break from work. I pulled my trusty popcorn popper from its home among my other favorite pots and pans. The doorbell rang, and Dashiell, barking and skittering around my couch, ran towards the door. I followed him at a more dignified pace. Solicitors are bound to call at mealtime but I've never known them to stop by in person. However, I played it safe and eyed my peephole. There on my stoop stood Lacey, hand poised over the buzzer.

I unlatched the door and she sprang inside. "Onalee, you've got to help us. Roy needs someone to take care of him and Pete can't do it, for obvious reasons. They

don't think it would be good for me to do
it either, just in case they—"

"Whoa. Slow down." Her words tumbled
on top of each other, and I was having
trouble keeping up with her. Also, Roy? And
Pete? "I thought Pete wasn't involved with
Roy."

She turned away. "Well, it turns out
he was, and none of them can keep him." She
looked back at me. "If the cops find out,
it will look really bad for Pete."

"Who's 'them'? And, where's Roy now?"
I was losing patience with her half-answers
that only raised more questions.

"Don't you get it? Pete and some of
his friends were over at Pembower's place.
They were going to free Roy."

"You mean steal him, don't you?"

Lacey sighed. "Whatever."

I sighed myself. *I'm getting too old
for twenty-something lingo.*

"Anyway, Pembower stormed out of his
house while they were doing it, and they
got in an epic fight. It was the same night
he got killed. So now if the police know
that Pete's group has Roy, they'll think
for sure that he did it."

"And did he?"

Hot Dog

She crossed her arms. "We've already had this conversation, Onalee. Of course not."

I too became an arm crosser and an eye narrower. "Where is Roy? And, how can you be so sure Pete didn't do it? When there are fights, tempers flare. People do things they normally wouldn't do."

Lacey sighed. "Anyway, Roy is still at one of the guy's house, but they're, like, going to take him to a cabin in the woods tonight. The trouble is, the cops are figuring out, one by one, who is in their group so they have to, like, get Roy out of the picture, and quickly."

"What does this have to do with me, Lacey?"

"We need you to go to the cabin a couple of times a day. You know, give Roy food and water and take him for walks?" She noticed my deepening glare. "Just quick walks so he can, you know, do his business. It won't take long."

"Why me? Why not Pete? Or, you for that matter?"

"The police are, like, watching their every move. Totally. Especially Pete's. And they're afraid they might be watching me now, too. Besides, I, like, work all day."

Ah, the old "You work at home so you must really be lollygagging around all day" sentiment.

"Actually, as a small business owner, I too work all the time, Lacey. I'd be hard pressed to find the time to go on far-flung visits to the hinterlands several times a day."

She looked down at the floor. "I know. I'm just, like, totally fried, I'm so worried. I didn't mean that you don't work. I just meant that I'm stuck in an office all day. I can't, like, leave in the middle of the afternoon. The cabin isn't too far away, and it would be an awesome drive this time of year." She looked up at me again and clasped her hands together. "Pleeeease, Onalee? Roy is such a sweet dog."

"Can't you guys just take him to the dog pound? He'd be looked after there, or is that too easy?"

"Do you realize how over-crowded they are? A dog like Roy, big, not like, really cute, and probably part German shepherd, nobody would adopt him. He'd be put to sleep in a matter of days."

"You must know someone else you can get to do this."

Hot Dog

"No, there's, like, nobody. The only other people we trust are either not dog lovers or they can't leave their jobs during the day. It would only be until this guy that Pete knows can get up here from downstate to take Roy away from here. In fact, I think he's coming this weekend."

"You think?"

"I'm, like, totally almost positive."

"All right. I'll do it until this weekend but that's it." I said, pleased with my no nonsense stance.

She broke into a smile. "Thanks, Onalee. I owe you. Big Time. Now, let me show you the map to the cabin. Pete wants him walked three times a day."

Chapter Eleven

The following morning as I motored into the hills east of town, I pondered the idea that maybe I wasn't as tough with Lacey as I'd thought. Following a sweeping curve high above the forests ringing a small lake, I knew that she was right about one thing, the drive out here was spectacular. The oranges and yellows created a muted backdrop for the showy scarlets of the red maples. Whether she was also correct about Pete's innocence, I wasn't so sure.

A couple of miles farther on, I turned down a narrow dirt lane that wound through the trees. I was pretty sure it was the right road. Soon I came upon a clearing with a rustic cabin. I pulled into the gravel drive and parked my car. What a pretty spot. A towering tree with its trunk twisting upwards was in front of the little cabin, its huge limbs partially sheltering it. The tree had an oriental look to it. I'd never seen one like it before, but its orange, saw-toothed leaves told me that it was some type of maple.

Hot Dog

Lacey had given me a key, and I fished it out of my pocket as I crossed the yard. I could hear barking coming from inside the house.

As soon as I opened the door, I spotted Roy. He hung back a little and watched me, ears up. Although we were acquainted, I didn't want to rush him. He'd been through some rough times at the hands of humans. I leaned down and held out a treat to him. His tail thumped against the floor and he edged over. He sniffed me and then reached out and snatched the morsel. I petted him on his shoulder and he moved in closer. I scratched and fondled his head around his ears and he sighed deeply. I think it was the doggie version of purring. "Ohhh, you sweet boy, you," I cooed.

"Wanna go for a walk?" A leash hung from a nail by the door. I attached it to his collar and opened the door. I thought we'd better avoid the road so we headed toward the rear of the house. A two-track led into the woods and we followed it. Roy was obviously trained to walk on a leash, and I wondered who had taken the time to do that. Surely not old sour apple Mr. Pembower. Roy took the opportunity for numerous leg lifts then meandered off the

trail and deposited a pile. That was one I
didn't bother to pick up.

I kicked through the leaves, enjoying
the feeling of the warm morning sunlight
filtering down through the forest. The
fallen foliage gave off a faintly musty
odor, the smell of autumn.

I wished I could let Roy off the leash
and watch him lope through the trees, but I
didn't know if he'd come back to me. I
couldn't risk it. We reached a place where
the path branched off both to the right and
the left. This was a smart place to turn
around. In the past, forking trails have
spelled disaster for this second-rate
pathfinder. We retraced our steps to the
little cabin.

Back inside, I poured dry dog food
into Roy's bowl and then got him some water
from the jugs stashed in the corner. The
cabin wasn't equipped with indoor plumbing
or running water. "Good bye, Roy. I'll be
back this afternoon and we'll go for
another little sashay." I petted him again.

* * *

I worked on my office building appraisal
for a couple of hours, went back out to
Roy's cabin again and then, guess what?
Time to take Dog Number-One, Dashiell, for

Hot Dog

his second walk of the day. *I'm sure glad I told Lacey in no uncertain terms that I would only take care of Roy-Boy until the weekend.*

* * *

I'd settled into a routine of numerous dog-walkings interspersed between appraisal duties. I thoroughly enjoyed my interludes with Roy but was looking forward to the time when I could get back to more productivity.

On Thursday afternoon, I hadn't seen or heard from Lacey since she'd talked me into this caper. Roy and I were strolling companionably back toward the cabin. As we broke out of the trees, Roy froze, and a growl gurgled in his chest. The hair on my arms stood up as I saw a man standing about 200 yards away.

He was too tall to be Pete, and besides, his arrogant stance looked disturbingly familiar to me. Granted, it wouldn't be propitious to be meeting up with a ruffian in this desolate woodland, a knave bent on burgling or worse. But I think I'd rather take my chances with such a fellow as that rather than the oh-so-smug Detective Costas.

Connie Doherty

I fought the urge to flee with Roy into the shelter of the nearby copse. But running would be pointless, and more importantly, undignified. Heads held high, Roy and I advanced toward our fate.

"Could that be you, Ms. O'Conner?"

"Yes, indeed it is. Mr. Costas, I presume?"

"It is he. If I could be so bold as to inquire, who is your friend?"

Time to improvise. I plastered a perplexed look on my face. "I'm not sure. I found him running in the road and caught up with him in yonder woods."

"I see," he said nodding his head. "Yet, he looks very much like a dog we've been searching for. A dog belonging to a murdered man." He paused, obviously toying with me. "I don't supposed you'd know anything about this, would you, Madam O'Conner?"

I heard a nervous trill of laughter escape my lips. "Now that you mention it, I do recall reading something about a man being killed. Maybe it's a good thing I rounded up this animal for you. He seems nice." I added as Roy and I continued to close the gap between Mr. Costas and ourselves.

Hot Dog

"What's your body count up to, Ms. O'Conner?" he asked dropping any pretense of niceness.

I stopped. The sun was in my eyes not allowing me to read the detective's face, but, I didn't like his tone of voice and wasn't about to humor him. Instead of answering his impertinent question, I said, "Recently I adopted a dog from a rescue, and happened to have a leash in my car. I'd be more than happy to keep this fellow at my house for a while, as long as he and Dashiell, my dog, get along okay." We'd continued pushing forward and were almost past him when the long arm of the lawman shot out and intercepted us.

"Hold it right there." Now that I could see his eyes, I wished I couldn't. They were boring right into me. "Enough games. I don't know how you happen to be connected to this crime but I'm going to find out. I'm taking you down to the station."

Chapter Twelve

And so it was that Roy and I found ourselves riding in the back of a police car, both of us careening toward uncertain futures.

Costas had examined Roy for tags, but to my knowledge the poor boy had never owned any. As we motored into town, he called an animal control officer and requested that he meet us at the station. When we pulled into the parking lot behind the police department, the truck was already there to carry Roy away and deposit him in limbo.

I sat there, not wanting to let go of him. I also knew enough about police cars to know that the back doors only open from the outside. I wasn't going to struggle with the door to the amusement of Mr. Costas. After a moment, the animal control guy opened the door nearest Roy.

"Hello, boy. Want to go for a ride?" Then he looked at me. "Do you want to hand me his leash, ma'am?"

Hot Dog

He seemed like a decent fellow, but I hated to see Roy go. "Please sir. He is such a nice dog. Make sure they treat him well," I said as I handed him the leash. My eyes were welling up. "How long will he have until they . . . they snuff him out?"

His eyes met mine. "They may not euthanize him. Hopefully, he'll find a good family and live the rest of his life in a warm and happy home."

"But if they don't? How long does he have?"

His eyes became troubled. "Generally it's ten days, ma'am."

"Okay. Thanks, Bill," Costas cut in. Turning to me he said, "Let's mosey along on into the station, Ms. O'Conner."

***

Costas grilled me for about an hour. I knew it was pointless to continue disavowing any knowledge of who Roy was, so I told him everything I knew. It was beginning to look very bad for Pete, but there was nothing I could do to help him. Costas had a frown on his face almost the entire time.

He eventually let me go with a strongly worded warning, something along the lines of keeping my nose out of official police business. *What an ill-*

tempered fellow he is! Later, when the crime remains unsolved, his pleas for my help will fall on deaf ears.

"Could I ask you one question?" I took his silence as a yes. "How did you find me, way out in the country?"

He gave me a feral grin. "By following your car. I figured you were up to your eyeballs in this."

"Oh." *I'd always wondered if I'd be able to detect a tail. Apparently, some of my skills were still un-sleuth-worthy.*

I forced myself to regroup. "Will it be you or one of your officers taking me back to my car . . . Camille?"

"Actually, we have a very reliable taxi service in this area. You may want to give them a call. Good day, Ms. O'Conner. Thanks for stopping in."

Costas turned on his heel and strode away, leaving me to find my own way back to the front door. I started down the corridor after Costas. After two wrong turns I doubled back. Proceeding down the hall to my right this time, I noted a poster about treating everyone with respect. I'd seen it on my way into this labyrinth. I must be on the right track, I thought. Soon, I would be within reach of the exit and sweet freedom. I made a sharp left and, "Uhgh."

"Oh my gosh. Are you all right?" The officer I'd slammed into reached out to steady me. "I'm so sorry, I guess my feet were flying while my head was in the clouds."

"I'm not sure who has the right of way around blind corners, but it's probably the guy with the gun."

His entire face crinkled into a wide grin. "Name's Donnely. Mitch Donnely," he said extending his hand again.

"Pleased to meet you. Onalee O'Conner here," I said as we shook hands.

"The Onalee O'Conner? I'm kind of new here, but I've heard of you." He mused for a moment. "I know. You're the Professional Petoskey Body Finder."

"I may have found a body or two, but none recently." I said demurely.

I could feel his eyes on me, but it wasn't at all unpleasant.

"The way Detective Costas talks about you, I had you pictured way different. Huh," he said, shaking his head. "Anyway, Onalee O'Conner, is there anything I can do for you now that we've run into each other?"

What was Commandant Costas saying about me that I would be pictured so differently than my real self? "Actually, I may be a bit turned around. Can you point me toward the front door?"

"Follow me," he said and led off in the direction from which I'd just come. As we walked along, he pointed out the indoor firing range and some of the other features of the building. After a couple more turns, he said, "There you are," and pointed to the door. "It was nice meeting you," he said and actually seemed to mean it.

"Thanks, and likewise." I gave him my sweetest smile. It was in my best interest to have at least one policeman in the ranks of the Costas force who was not repulsed on sight by yours truly.

I exited the front door and began the long walk home. I would have to ask Lacey or Ginger to give me a ride back out to the cabin for my car.

* * *

Nothing builds an appetite like being hauled into a police station, spilling one's guts and then hoofing it two miles home. I wolfed down two steaming bowls of chili. Lacey called as I was licking my spoon.

"Onalee. They've arrested Pete again. His roommate says they found Roy, too. What happened?"

It seemed to me that her tone was slightly accusatory, and after all I'd been through for that dame and her cockamamie friends. "Lacey, somehow or other the cops found out about the cabin and showed up while I was there. I was at the police station all morning, cooling my heels."

"You didn't tell them anything, did you?"

"Yes, I told them the truth. If that somehow implicates Pete then I can't help it. And by the way, my car is still at the cabin. I need a ride out there to get it."

"Um. I can't tonight. I'm, like, supposed to go—"

"Lacey!"

"Okay. How about at 6:00, right after I get off work?"

* * *

Later that evening I was relaxing with a good book as Dashiell slept in his auxiliary bed. I heard occasional muffled woofs, and his feet twitched as he galloped through the meadows of dreamland. The phone startled us both, and I jumped to answer it.

"Hi, On. Long time no talk to."

"Marti. This is a surprise. What's up? You're not calling to tell me some great news like, to save a certain date in June, are you?"

"Quit rushing us, On. Frank is in no hurry to tie the knot, and neither am I."

"And you call me a commitment-phobe. Are you going to wait until you can both draw Social Security together?"

"Ha, ha. Frank is going to be in Ohio for a training session for a week. I don't have any imminent appraisal deadlines, so it would be a perfect time for me to come for a little visit."

Uh-oh. Marti's little visits have spelled big trouble for me in the past. Her over-active adventure gland is the problem. "Ordinarily, I'd love to see you, but things have been kind of crazy up here and—"

"You know me, On. I can entertain myself. I plan to hit the road about eight o'clock, so I should be rolling in about noon. I've got to go, so see you then. Bye."

I stared at the phone. This couldn't be a good thing, but there was nothing I could do about it. Dashiell and I took our last walk of the night and went to bed.

Chapter Thirteen

At about one o'clock the following day, Marti strolled up to my front door with a giant ficus plant. Dashiell barked and the doorbell rang as I quickly saved everything on my computer and dashed to the door. Marti rolled her suitcase in, set the plant in the window, flopped on the couch and demanded to be "brought up to speed on our case."

Oh, no. Once again we'll stick our noses into the dark underbelly of Northern Michigan. Then she'll waltz back home to the safety of Detroit, and I'll be the one left by myself, fending off Jack or Jackie-the-Ripper.

However, no one can stop Ms. Gonzalez on a mission, so while she fondled Dashiell's ears, I filled her in on the latest evil afflicting our fair city.

"Who have you interrogated to this point?"

"You think I just willy-nilly stopped my appraisal practice and slid into private eye mode?"

Hot Dog

"There are twenty-four hours in every single day. You ought to be able to manage both, Missy."

Arghghhgh. "Speaking of which, I was right in the middle of typing a description of the office building I'm working on. I'd better get back at it."

"That's fine. I'm up here for some R and R. Work has been crazy lately. I brought the latest Peg Herring book with me and I'll hang out here on your couch for a while and read."

I glanced at the cover. "Ooh, the fourth Sleuth Sisters mystery. Can I borrow it when you're done?"

"Sure. Now, get back to work."

***

Around three o'clock, Marti, Dashiell and I went for an uneventful walk. With no great need to play hostess for Marti, we ate left-over lentil soup for dinner. As we cleaned up the kitchen, Marti circled back to the "Pembower Affair" as she'd dubbed it. "I've been thinking, On. I'll bet your friend Susan would be a good person to talk with. You said she lives right by the guy. Let's go there tonight."

***

There were lights on in the house Susan had pointed out to me the day Pembower's body had been found. We hadn't called, because I didn't have her phone number and only knew her as Susan the dog-walker. We stood on the porch after the doorbell sounded and heard Riley barking. Soon Susan opened the door.

"Onalee, what a surprise!" Smiling, she looked at me, then at Marti. I introduced them, and we were invited in to her compact ranch-style home. The front door opened into her living room. The television was on, and Riley sprawled out on the sofa, intently following the action on the screen. I went over to him and, tail thumping, he made eye contact with me for a brief moment before turning his attention back to the TV.

Susan shook her head. "In the past I always lost the men in my life to the boob tube. When I rescued Riley from the shelter, I thought I'd have a real companion." She sighed. "Can I get either of you a glass of wine or anything?"

"We brought over a bottle. Do you like Merlot?" Marti asked pulling a bottle out of a shopping bag.

"Sure. I'll get my opener."

Hot Dog

Soon, Marti and I were sitting in a couple of easy chairs while Susan shared the couch with Riley. As the wine flowed, we chatted about all of the dogs and dog people we had in common. As a clever segue into the "Pembower Affair", I told Susan about my adventures taking care of Roy.

"I'm so glad to hear that he's okay, at least for now. I wondered what happened to him."

"It turns out that Pete and a few of his friends were at Pembower's house the night he was offed. They were trying to take Roy and got in a big fight with Mr. P." I paused to let her digest that information while I sipped my wine. "Did you hear anything unusual that night?"

She rubbed Riley's neck as he rested his head on her leg. "The police asked me that, and no I didn't. But, I'm a pretty sound sleeper."

"This might make Pete one of the leading suspects," I said.

"Do you believe he did it?"

"Lacey doesn't think so."

"Yeah, but she's got a crush on him, doesn't she?" A commercial came on, and Riley jumped up and bounded into the kitchen. A few minutes later, water dripped from his muzzle as he clambered back on the couch beside Susan.

Marti and I exchanged a glance. "She does, but I have to say he doesn't strike me as the cold-blooded killer type, either," I said.

"You live practically on top of the crime scene, Susan. Who do you think did it?" The on-task Ms. Gonzalez asked.

"I don't think any of us neighbors have actually been taken off the suspect list, but if you ask me, I would look towards his ex-wife. He was terrible to her. He beat her up . . . a lot."

"Wow. What a heel," I said.

Susan nodded. "The times we got into it, he scared me. More than once I thought he was going to hit me. I think part of me kind of hoped he would so I could send him to jail for assault."

I felt a shiver run through me. "No, no. You don't need that kind of trouble."

"How do we find the ex-wife if we want to talk to her?"

Susan turned to Marti. "Why would you want to talk with her?"

"Marti is a self-described amateur detective," I said to explain my friend's behavior.

"Oh."

"As you may remember, Onalee and I worked a case about a year and a half ago that resulted in our apprehension of a murderer."

Hmmmn. Is that the way Marti remembers it? She was involved on the periphery but . . . "our" apprehension of the murderer?

"Is that true?" Susan asked me.

"Basically, I guess."

"Now that another murder has fallen into our laps, we need to take steps to solve it," announced Marti.

"Won't the police be upset if you interfere?"

"Initially. But they—"

Suddenly woofing erupted from the television. Riley leaped to his feet, and standing about a yard from the TV, began barking furiously at the on-air canine. Susan hit the remote control, and the set shut off. Riley spun around to face her, continuing his tirade.

"Riley, no! Bad boy!" She shouted, to no avail. She looked over at us. "He knows I'm not a dog-hitter and my yelling at him does nothing. Got any ideas?"

Marti and I both shook our heads.

"Well, this usually works," she said,

turning the TV back on. Screen-dog was gone and Riley hopped back on the couch, laid down and crossing his front paws, emitted a small sigh.

"As I was saying, Marti continued, "At first, the police think we're a bit of a bother. But they recognize solid detective work when they see it."

"Onalee, your eyes are as round as saucers. Are you okay?" Susan asked.

I swung my head around from Marti and nodded. "Yup. It's just that this is the first time I've heard my sidekick's take on the investigation we executed."

Marti glared at me. "Sidekick. I am not sidekick material. Even though you were technically the 'boots on the ground', you know good and well that I headed up that inquiry." She turned back to Susan, "As I was saying. If you know how we can get in touch with the ex-Mrs. Pembower, it would be a great help."

"I heard she was in an apartment." She looked up and to her left then shook her head. "I can't remember the name."

"I'm pretty familiar with a lot of the apartments around here. Where are they located?" *Appraising apartments is almost as much fun as industrial buildings.*

Hot Dog

"Um. Back behind Tinselman's."

"I know where you mean. Amesbury Lane Apartments."

Susan pointed at me. "That's the one."

"What else do you know about her? How long have they been estranged? Is she remarried? Do they—"

"Whoa", Susan laughed. "I can see why you two make good detectives. I'll try to answer your questions, Marti, but I don't keep in touch with her. I didn't go out of my way to be friendly with her while she was here, because of her creepy husband, Gerald. Anyway, as far as I know, she moved out a couple of years ago. Their kids were long gone by then. I assume they got a divorce, but I don't know for sure. I heard she was with a guy but maybe she's just living with him."

"Does she work anywhere?" I asked. "That's a pretty big apartment complex. It'll be hard to track her down if she isn't in the phone book. And what's her first name?"

"Now you're double-teaming me." She looked back and forth between the two of us, smiling.

I guess anyone who could put up with a dog like Riley wouldn't get too rattled by me and Marti, or apparently I should say, Marti and her sidekick.

Susan got up and divided the last of the wine into our three glasses. "I'll tell you one thing. I will never let Riley have any wine. I think he'd be a mean drunk." He looked at her and thumped his tail against the couch, knowing she was talking about him. "You're my sweet doggie," she said smoothing the hair between his eyes. Looking back at us, she said, "Gerald's ex is named Sharon. The last I knew, she worked at the dry cleaners on the west side of town, Carthmore's or some name like that."

"I know the one you mean."

"Which of the neighbors do you think we should talk to?" Marti asked.

"Because they might be suspects?"

Marti nodded.

"Let's see. Nobody liked the guy, but that's different than being willing to kill him. Remember, Onalee, when I told you about our neighbor Dick who got in a yelling match with him when Dick's boy went in Pembower's yard? He has nothing good to say about Pembower, but I can't imagine Dick getting violent. Actually, I would suspect that all of us got in a fight with

Hot Dog

Gerry at one time or another. I can give you the names of my neighbors and you could go door to door and talk with them.

"Great," I said, brightly. "You could initiate that ground work tomorrow while I get some appraising done, Gumshoe Gonzalez."

"Even though you're palming off your grunt work, O'Conner, I'll happily shoulder the burden if it will further our understanding of this case."

Riley's program wound up, and Susan flicked her wrist to check out the time as surreptitiously as possible. I stood up. "It's getting late, and Marti and I have big days ahead of us tomorrow. Thanks, Susan." We retrieved our jackets from the entryway closet and made our way out into the now rainy night.

* * *

The following morning found us in the middle of a downpour. Of course Dashiell and I made our rounds, but Marti stayed in her cozy bed on the air mattress in my living room. She was on her second cup of coffee when we left. As far as I was concerned, any amateur detective worth her salt would have cheerfully sauntered out

into the deluge in the off chance that a
suspect or two was about.

Chapter Fourteen

The Dashmeister and I slogged down the street and into the parking lot by the bike path. The little Mustang convertible was parked, as usual, at the far end. We traipsed onto the beach and along the water's edge for about ten minutes. The wind-driven rain pounded the sand and we were both drenched. We'd had enough and turned around to make our way back. As we did, the rain let up.

At the parking lot, we veered toward the Mustang. If Ms. Gonzalez is going to do some sleuthing, maybe I should work the program as well, I thought. The man was awake, and put his book down as I approached. He may be hoping for another cache of cans, I thought. He opened the window a couple of inches. "Hi," I said. "We kind of met the other day."

"I remember. Thanks for the cans."

"You're welcome. I was wondering if . . . you're here quite a bit. What do you know about some of the other people around here?"

He looked away for a moment and then turned back, "Like who?"

I leaned towards the window a bit but he moved away, so I straightened back up. "There's a fellow with a long beard who rides his bike around here."

A small smile crossed the man's face. "You mean Tommy, my competition." He looked up at me again. "He collects bottles, too."

"Oh. I've never seen him do that."

"Why are you interested in him?"

"I saw the cops take him away the day the man was murdered not too far from here."

"And you're wondering if he did it?"

"Do you think he did?"

"I have no idea. He doesn't seem to be violent." He paused in thought. "Although, one time I did see him get in a fight with the guy in the black truck that used to park here all the time. That man was really hassling him though. Calling him a bum. Threatening to call the cops. He caught Tommy going through the recycling bins up the way there." He pointed towards the metal bins at the other end of the parking lot.

"What's wrong with that?"

Hot Dog

"You're not supposed to do it, though we all do, looking for cans and bottles. Personally, I think the only reason they don't want us to is because the recycle-workers want those returnables to line their pockets." He shook his head. "We need the dough more than they do. They've got decent jobs. We've got squat."

"Maybe it's because of safety issues and liability. So, they got into it?" I asked, hoping he'd give me more details.

"Yeah. The truck guy is a real scum bucket. I don't know who appointed him governor, but he got out of his truck and slammed Tommy against one of the big containers. I think he would've hauled off and slugged him, but a couple of cars pulled in to the parking lot right then. I don't think he wanted to be seen beating a homeless person to a pulp." He paused. "He shoved him again into the bin then just walked away like nothing had happened and got back in his truck. Tommy stayed there for the longest time and then kind of slunk away. I felt bad for him. He didn't do anything to deserve that."

"That's awful," I said. "Any idea who the man in the truck is? I haven't seen him around here lately."

"Me either, but, I'll tell you one thing, I'm not going to stick around if I do. That guy is vicious."

"Have you talked to Tommy since then?"

"Naw. He's not big on chitchat."

"How do you know his name?"

"His buddy Ron. Ever seen him around? He's a younger guy. Reddish hair. Better dressed. You see him on the bike path, walking back and forth between town and here. He also goes down to the beach."

"That kind of rings a bell."

"He and Tommy hang out together sometimes. Ron will talk your arm off."

"I'm sorry. I've never introduced myself. I'm Onalee O'Conner and this is Dashiell."

"I'm Michael." He gave me a small smile. "Nice to meet you." Then he shifted the book he'd been reading in his hands. It looked like our interview was over.

"I'd better get going. Thanks for the info."

Michael sketched a wave then rolled up his window. I'd almost said I'd better head home but I caught myself just in time. That would have been a terrible thing to say to a homeless person. Poor guy. I wondered how he'd wound up having to live in his car.

Hot Dog

Meanwhile, back at the cozy O'Conner estate, it appeared that Ms. Gonzalez had done nothing more than turn a few pages of her novel during Dashiell's and my absence.

"Hi, On. Still raining out?" she asked, her eyes never leaving the book.

"No, it's nippy, though. When did you plan to stir your stumps, Ms. G?"

Her head swung up. "I think I'll stay put for a while, since I can't put this book down. After lunch is when I'll start my reconnoitering."

I snapped off Dashiell's leash. "Sounds good. What's the plan?"

"What I was thinking was that you could drive me over to the crime scene so I could get a feel for the lay of the land. From there, I could fan out and talk to the neighbors."

"Okie-doke" I said as I slipped into the inner sanctum of O'Conner Appraisal, Ltd, and went back to work on my office building. I know there are appraisers who enjoy valuing offices, but to me they are usually boring. If problems pop up with them, and they do from time to time, they become downright irritating.

Take for instance my subject property. The owner bought the building five years ago for about eighty dollars per square foot. Then he turned around and plowed another one hundred dollars per square foot into it. As my dad used to say, "He built a monument to himself." The building is located in a little town in the hinterlands of the boonies. They have one stop light. In the whole county.

Comparable office building sales that were also located in far-flung-villes topped out at about ninety dollars per square foot, and they were almost as nice as the property I was appraising. Nobody was going to be happy with this appraisal.

I persevered at my thankless task until lunchtime, then Marti and I broke bread and peanut butter together. Afterwards, we threw on our winter parkas, hats and gloves before hitting the trail. I piloted the Honda down the familiar street running by Pembower's side yard and parked across from it. The house was closed up and still vacant. I wondered what the family would do with it.

I showed Marti where poor Roy had been staked out. Obviously I couldn't show her the actual crime scene, since it had taken place inside the house, but I filled her in on the details I knew. According to newspaper accounts, he'd been killed by his own hand-gun. Police theorized that Pembower had fought with his assailant and eventually been overcome.

From where we parked, we could see the residence to the east and one to the north with an adjacent backyard. According to Susan, Dick, who had gotten in a fight with Pembower, lived in the house to the north. A retired school teacher lived in the house immediately east.

A black sedan coming from the west, slowed as it drew abreast of my Honda. "Uh-oh."

Chapter Fifteen

Marti craned her neck to see out my window. "Who is it, On?"

"Um." His window slid down, and he gestured for me to open mine.

"Ms. O'Conner." The icy words slid off his tongue. "What brings you out to these environs?"

"Hello, Detective. I was just showing my friend Marti here around the city. She's from downstate."

He peered into the car.

"Hi. I'm Marti Gonzalez. I'm up visiting Onalee from Detroit."

"Pleased to meet you. I'm Detective Costas. I'm afraid Ms. O'Conner is giving you short shrift. Our neighborhoods, such as this one, though safe and pretty, are relatively unremarkable. We have a lovely waterfront area that I believe you'd enjoy more. Also, I'd like to suggest the drive to Cross Village along the shore road. It's stunning this time of the year."

Marti's dimples deepened as her smile blazed at the detective. "Thank you. It's always good to get suggestions from people who live in the area."

In spite of himself, Costas grinned at Marti the Enchantress. When he turned back to me, things got ugly again. "It's quite astounding how you happen to turn up at crime scenes, Ms. O. Explain to me, in fifty words or less, what you're doing parked outside the Pembower house." In an aside to Marti, he said, "In case you're not aware, Miss Gonzalez, your friend Onalee is famous in these parts for sticking her nose into official police business."

"Detective, Onalee might be a little over-zealous sometimes. Ever since her boyfriend Rick broke up with her, I'm afraid she has too much time on her hands. But I'll talk to her about it."

My jaw dropped as my head swung around to stare at Marti the Treacherous.

"I'd appreciate that, Marti. Ms. O'Conner, you run along now and show your guest the beauties of Northern Michigan." With that, the Costas mobile eased forward.

Marti immediately started in, "He's cute, Onalee, and I can tell he's got a crush on you."

My mouth finally clamped shut. I was too ticked to retort at that moment.

"Drop me off at the house and I'll bring my car back over here and start talking with the neighbors," quoth the oblivious Ms. G.

***

I plunged ahead on my appraisal all afternoon, breaking only to take Dashiell on his three o'clock walk. Afterwards I placed my daily phone call to the dog pound to see how Roy Boy was doing. He was still an inmate there but doing well, they told me. My last caregiving activity involved sloshing some water over the infernal ficus. *Nasty thing. Taking up space in my house but not paying any rent. As soon as Marti leaves, this flora will find itself curbside. People know better than to give unsolicited puppies or kittens. Yet, they think nothing of palming off plants on their friends.*

At 5:00 I started stirring up a pot of navy bean soup. I couldn't believe that Marti wasn't back yet. *Maybe I should take a drive over to Pembower-ville again. If she's not back by 5:30, that's what I'll do.* I finished peeling and dicing potatoes and the soup was simmering by the time she showed up. She'd been gone all afternoon. I had to admit that her stick-to-it-iveness was impressive.

***

"Hi, On."

"Belly on up to the bar there and I'll pour you a glass of wine. Dinner will be ready in about an hour."

Marti shrugged out of her jacket and hopped up on one of my barstools as I poured us some cabernet.

"What did you find out?"

Marti took a sip. "Good wine, On. What kind is this?"

I shoved the bottle over closer to her. "Three bucks a bottle and it's from Spain. So? You made the rounds?" I prompted.

"Kind of. Not many people home. I did talk with Mrs. Marstead, the school teacher. She was nice."

"What did you learn from her?"

"That the young people of today don't have time for their elders. That we're all going to hell in a hand basket. Or is it hen basket? I never know which."

"Hand basket. I looked it up one time. What did she say about Pembower?"

"She'd had one of his kids in school and knew the family was going to be trouble when they moved in to the neighborhood."

"Did she have any problem with him?" I pressed. The normally loquacious Marti was keeping her thoughts awfully close to the vest.

"Mainly she complained about the loud music. She said she never called the police, but it kept her awake a lot of nights." Marti toyed with her wine glass. "On, you're not mad at me still, are you?"

I wished she hadn't brought that up. Now I felt my ire rising all over again. "I could've killed you for saying that stuff to Costas."

"Yeah, I know. Afterwards, I thought maybe I went a teeny bit too far. But, honestly, On. He is cute and I can tell he likes you."

"Yeah, about as much as a case of ptomaine poisoning."

"You're wrong about that. He just didn't realize you were available." She looked into my eyes. "And, I think he's really shy."

"Costas? Are you kidding me? He is the most arrogant man who has ever crossed my path."

"No, you've got him wrong. Anyway, are we okay?"

I took in her earnest expression. Maybe I could turn this to my advantage. "If you promise to take that free-loading ficus with you when you leave, then I'd say we're even. But, in the future, keep your mitts out of my love life." I snorted for emphasis. "Now, getting back to your interviews."

"That's about it."

"What? You were gone for nearly four hours."

"Like I said, nobody was home. It's a weekday. There was one other guy home but he wouldn't give me the time of day. I finally gave up and moseyed on downtown to check out the stores. That reminds me. I bought you some fresh ground coffee from the restaurant on Lake Street. We can have it tomorrow."

"That's it? You only interviewed one person?"

"Yeah, but I'll get to more of them tomorrow. They should all be home on Saturday morning. In fact, you can go with me."

"Wrongo. Some people are still ruled by deadlines around here. This appraisal

was due at 5:00 today. But as you well
know, an appraisal emailed before Monday at
8:00 a.m. is equal to one that gets there
at 5:00 p.m. on Friday."

"That's always been my rule too. Do
you think the bankers are good with that?"

"I don't see why they wouldn't be. If
it comes in at 4:45 Friday, they won't open
it up until Monday morning anyway. Want a
tad more wine?"

"Sure." She breathed in deeply. "That
soup smells wonderful, On.

There is nothing like simmering
onions, garlic, bay leaves and thyme on a
fall day, I thought.

***

The following morning Marti and I savored
the coffee she'd purchased along with a
batch of white chocolate chip peanut butter
muffins I'd stirred up the evening before.
Then we took Dashiell on his rounds. Other
than meeting up with Lacey and Kitty, our
walk was uneventful. Lacey regaled us with
her most recent kitchen disaster.

"I'd always thought those exploding
baked potatoes were an urban myth," I said.

"I wish. I'm not sure I'll ever, like,
get that spud-crud off the walls of the

oven. Hey, Onalee, you promised me a cooking lesson, remember?"

"Yes, I did. I should be finished with this appraisal at some point today." I turned to Marti. "What do you think? Are you up for teaching a tyro a thing or two about kitchen techniques tomorrow?"

"As long as all I have to do is eat and maybe drink a glass or two of wine, I'm in."

***

After lunch, I dove back into my appraisal while Marti hit the mean streets. This time she was able to connect with the neighbor named Dick. He confirmed what Susan had told us about his run in with Pembower. He also said that the coroner had estimated the time of death at between 2:00 and 5:00 a.m. He'd been home asleep with his family. The police had questioned him and all of the neighbors, as far as he knew.

Marti also talked with three of Pembower's other neighbors. No one had heard or seen anything that night, or so they said. The only thing Girl Friday learned that Saturday was that nobody was wallowing in grief at the man's untimely death. After a few hours of sleuthing, she

circled back to the house in time to go for
Dashiell's afternoon walk.

* * *

The following afternoon, Lacey and Kitty
were at my house by 4:00 sharp. How some
people can be so punctual is beyond the ken
of this appraiser. Dashiell and Kitty ran
around in circles, thrilled at being
together at an unexpected time.

"So, Lacey, before you take your coat
off, what should we make for dinner? We
may need to go to the store for a few
supplies."

She scrunched her shoulders up. "Like,
I don't know." She gave me a blank look.
"Whatever."

I saw that I needed to take charge
here, as Marti looked on, amused. "How
hungry are you? Some things take longer
than others."

"I'm not, like, starved or anything,"
she said.

"Okay. We could make pizza. I usually
figure on about an hour to do that. How
does that sound?"

She broke into a big grin. "Really? I
could learn to make pizza? Isn't that,
like, super complicated with yeast and
everything?"

Hot Dog

"Easy, peasy, even though we will be working with yeast. Want to try it?"

She pumped her fist. "Yeah. Cool."

"I think I have everything we need for that unless you want anchovies on your third of the pie."

"Ewww."

Marti and I both chuckled. "All righty then. To the spoons we go," I said, marching towards my kitchen.

I got my recipe, bowls, and measuring cups. I explained to Lacey about reading through the entire recipe before starting. "I hate it when I get part-way along and have to stop and run out for a missing ingredient."

While she read, I pulled out flour, yeast and other ingredients and lined them up on my counter. "Do we have everything?" I asked her.

She studied my line up. "I don't see tomato paste."

"Ha, ha. I guess I forgot to get that out."

She gave me a sharp look and then laughed. "You were testing me, weren't you?"

"On is tricky like that, Lacey. You've got to watch her."

I dug out a small can of paste and then said, "Okay, Lacey. Show us what you're made of." I extended my arm towards the loaded counter.

She whirled around to face me, "You want me to do it? I'll wreck it. I don't know how." A bit of a whine crept into her voice.

"No, you won't. Marti and I will be right here beside you. Now pick up that cup and start measuring. Why don't you start with the flour?"

She reached out for one of the measuring cups and pulled the canister of flour forward.

"Although you could use that one, it's actually for measuring liquids." I picked up the other cup. This one is the best to use for flour because you can get a pretty exact measurement by scraping the excess off with a knife. I scooped out a cup for her and then she measured the rest of the flour and the other dry ingredients.

"Now you're ready for the yeast."

She picked up the packet of yeast and was just about to dump it into the bowl with the flour.

Hot Dog

"Whoa, girl." I couldn't help laughing. "Didn't your mama teach you nothin' about cooking?"

She turned towards me, her face clouded over. "My mom was a great mother, but she never taught me anything about, like, cooking or cleaning. Now she's dead."

"Oh, Lacey, I'm sorry." I reached out and hugged her.

She wiped up a couple of tears that had spilled from her eyes. "That's okay. You didn't know." She looked at me. "How old are you? Maybe you knew my Mom. She grew up around here."

"I'm 45."

"Seriously? That's like, how old my Mom would be. Did you know Nancy Barden?"

"Oh my gosh!" I yelped. "You're Nance's daughter? We used to walk to school together every day. We went to different colleges after high school and somehow lost touch. She's dead?" I asked, still in a state of disbelief.

"Yes. Last year. I miss her every day."

"I've thought about your mom so many times. We had a lot of fun together when we were little." I shook my head. "I guess I always thought we'd run into each other somewhere down the line." I could feel that my own eyes were glistening with tears. I studied her. "Now that I think about it, you look like your mom."

"People used to tell me that all the time."

"Who is your dad? Was he from here as well?"

"No, they met at Michigan State, but my mom and dad got divorced when I was ten. He got, like, a new family and never had time for me after that."

"Lacey, sweetie." Marti said and she gave her a hug.

Lacey swiped at her eyes again and turned to me. "It's epic that you knew my mom. Wow!"

"She was a wonderful person." I sighed. "Now, let me show you what to do with that yeast."

As we finished constructing the pizza and put it in the oven, Lacey told us about moving to Petoskey after college because her grandmother was here. Then she died, leaving Lacey all alone. Meanwhile, she had fallen in love with northern Michigan and planned to stay. Over a second glass of wine, the discussion turned to guys. Marti talked about her main squeeze, Frank.

Hot Dog

"How'd you guys meet?" Lacey asked.

"He was the prime suspect in the arson case she cracked," I said.

Marti glared at me. "He was not the prime suspect. Well, maybe he was at first, but we were able to quickly clear his name."

Lacey's eyes rounded. "You proved him innocent and then fell in love. Awesome."

"Something like that, yeah." Marti smiled.

I shook my head, remembering the affair quite a bit differently. Then I turned towards Lacey. "What's Pete up to tonight?" I asked hoping for some news of that amour.

"Hanging out with some of his buddies."

"Are you two an item, now?"

She looked at me quizzically. "What? You mean, like, have we hooked up?"

"Yeah, I guess so."

"You know, I think maybe he's the one," she said and a dreamy look swept over her eyes.

"He seems like a nice guy, but—"

Her head jerked up. "But, what?"

"It's all that dog stealing stuff. What exactly is he into, do you know?"

"He's, like, a huge dog lover, and he can't stand to see an animal in trouble."

"That's all well and good, but if what he's doing is illegal, then it's very risky."

"Don't worry, he's totally careful."

"What about the night at Pembower's house?"

"That was unusual."

"I like Pete, but it's you I'm worried about. I just don't want to see you get in over your head."

"Okay, Mom." She smiled at me. "I'll watch out for myself."

I knew she was kidding, but a warm glow spread over me as my old friend Nancy's daughter called me mom. She was all alone in the world, and I would do my best to keep her safe, as Nancy would have done for me.

I took a spatula out and lifted the pizza to check for brownness. It was done. "Lacey. I always give Dashiell a little pizza. Can Kitty have some?"

"Sure. She loves it."

After all five of us plowed through what we could of the pizza, there was enough left over for everyone's dinner the next night. Lacey left soon after the

Hot Dog

kitchen clean-up. Marti and I trotted
around the neighborhood with Dashiell and
then pulled out our paperbacks and pj's.
About 8:00 the telephone rang. An unknown
number showed up on caller ID.

Chapter Sixteen

"Hello. Can I speak to Onalee? This is Mitch Donnely."

The name sounded familiar. "Oh, you're a c . . . policeman, right?"

"Yup. I met you at the station."

"Sure, I remember."

"I know this is short notice, but tomorrow is supposed to be in the mid-fifties and sunny. I've got the day off and wondered if you'd like to go for a bike ride."

Hmmmn. My appraisal was finished. I had scheduled miscellaneous office work for the next day. I was deadline free for a change. The guy had gone out of his way for me the other day and he was cute, I mused. *It's not like there are hordes of men battering down my door for a chance to woo me.* "Sounds good. When and where?"

"You'll really go? Great," he said excitedly. "I was thinking about two o'clock, but if that doesn't work for you—"

"No, two is fine."

Hot Dog

"I'll swing by your house and we can go from there."

Marti's book was lying open, and she was sitting up in her air-bed straining to catch every word. "Sounds good, I'll see you then. Wait. Do you know where I live?"

"Of course. I'm a cop, remember?"

I put the phone back in its cradle and sauntered towards my bedroom.

"Stop right there, Missy. Who was that and where are you going at 2:00?"

"It was a guy I met last week. He seems nice but I don't know him too well. We're going for a bike ride tomorrow. No biggy."

"No 'biggy'? How long has it been since you went anywhere with a guy? And didn't 'biggy' go out twenty years ago?"

"I don't know exactly how long it's been since I've been with anyone. It's not like I've had enough time on my hands to obsess over such things. Lastly, I'll curb my use of 'biggy' now that I know that the speech police are in town."

"Humph. I need details. He's a cop? What's his name? Is he cute?"

There was nothing like the promise of a little romance to revitalize Ms. Gonzalez. "He is a policeman, his name's

Mitch, and he's pretty decent looking. Have I covered everything?"

"When is your date? Tomorrow?"

"It's not a date. It's a bike ride. And yes, it is tomorrow. Want to come with us?"

"Are you kidding? I'm sure Mitcharoonie would love that."

"It's just a bike ride. He said it was going to be warm tomorrow, so it'd be a great day for you to go."

She declined again. We said our good nights, and I read fifteen or twenty pages of my book. Meanwhile, from the living room came soft murmurs as Marti had her nightly chat with Far-away Frank.

* * *

The following afternoon, Mitch turned into my driveway at about ten minutes after 2:00. A guy who is late to his first date. I like that in a man. He lifted his bike off the rack and then came to the door. I stepped away from the window and answered the bell.

"Hi, Onalee. We've got a gorgeous day for this," he grinned. "Ready to roll?"

My bike was parked on the sidewalk. "Sure," I said as I shut and locked the door.

Hot Dog

It was close to sixty degrees and sunny. To our sun-starved bodies, it felt like a summer day. We followed the bike path into town. Between Petoskey and Bay Harbor, the trail arches up along a cliff overlooking Little Traverse Bay. Sapphire waters stretched to the horizon.

We learned a little about each other as we pedaled part of the way to Charlevoix before turning around. On our way back, we pushed our bikes as we raced across the highway to the Speckled Pickle, a local deli and favorite of yours truly and Mitch, too, as it turned out. We carried our sandwiches and iced teas to the back deck, not wanting to waste any of the waning daylight.

I watched as Mitch took a large bite of his sandwich and closed his eyes. "Hmmm. Hmmm." He said, obviously in rapture.

The sandwiches were about four inches thick, but Mitch easily wrapped his lips around it. I hadn't thought through the logistics of the giant sandwiches as well as I should have. Always before, I had taken my lunch home and eaten it in the privacy of my kitchen. On a first date/bike ride there are certain faux pas that need to be avoided. Memo to self: avoid behemoth sandwiches until at least month three in a relationship.

"Aren't you hungry? You haven't touched a bite."

"I am. I'm just gearing up to chow down." I pinched the sandwich parts together with all my might as I glommed on with my teeth. Some part of the innards refused to succumb to my gnashing teeth and I was forced to give my head a quick shake in order to tear the preternaturally tough green thing in two. As it slid out, along with it cascaded chunks of avocado and tahini dressing, forcing me to gulp them down with rapid mastication.

After mastering these mouthfuls, I looked over at Mitch, who was studying the trees along the back of the property. I took a quick swipe of my face with a napkin and felt my composure returning.

Mitch's head swiveled back towards me. "I'm so glad you were willing to play hooky today. This would've been a boring ride by myself."

"Friends don't let friends bike alone."

As he laughed his eyes crinkled and I suddenly hoped he'd call me again. I could call him, but from my nearly thirty years

of dating experience, I've noted that early
on in a relationship, it never pays for the
woman to call the man. Of course this
observation probably holds true only for my
generation, give or take ten years.

We hopped back on our bikes for the
final leg of our journey. I'd taken my
jacket off earlier, but clouds had
overtaken the sun and a chill wind had
sprung up.

"Hey, Mitch. I'm going to stop and put
my parka back on."

"I was thinking the same thing."

We were on a part of the bike path
that ran adjacent to the highway. Traffic
was heavy as our Northern Michigan version
of rush hour progressed. Side by side,
Mitch and I stood astride our bikes and
donned our gear as a familiar black auto
motored by. Mitch waved and received a
light horn honk in return.

"Was that Costas?"

"Yup, the detective himself."

* * *

Marti, Dashiell and I walked the beach the
following morning. It was sunny and 72
degrees. Marti and I were in shorts and tee
shirts. A gentle southwesterly breeze
buffeted us as small waves lapped the

shore. We lingered, soaking up the spectacular day. Surprisingly, we didn't run into any two or four-legged creatures other than a couple of squirrels. When we got back to the house, my telephone my phone was ringing.

"Onalee. It's Lacey. I'm, like, in jail."

Chapter Seventeen

"Lacey! What happened?"

"It's kind of, like, a long story, but could you come down here? I'm not sure how long they're going to keep me, and I need someone to take care of Kitty."

"I'll be right there."

Marti and I jumped into my car and sped to the police station.

Lucky for me, neither Costas nor Mitch Donnely were around. When we were finally allowed to see her, Lacey looked terrible. Mascara smudges around her eyes showed she'd been crying. When she looked up at us from the table where she was seated, tears welled up again. I bent over her and gave her a chair hug. "What happened, Sweetie?"

She hung her head. "I—I might not have told you everything," she said and wiped her eyes with the back of her hand.

Marti and I both shot her piercing looks as we took chairs beside her. I had a bad feeling about this. "Lacey? What haven't you told us?"

"You know that night that Pembower
died?"

"Yes," I said.

"And, Pete, like, tried to steal Roy?"

"Spit it out Lacey," said Get-To-The-
Point-Gonzalez.

Lacey looked back and forth between
us. Marti heaved a sigh.

Lacey's head hung even lower. Speaking
to the table, I thought she said, "I was
there with him."

"You were at Pembower's the night he
got killed?" I shouted as I leaned in
towards her.

"Yes, but we didn't do it." She looked
up at me. "You've got to believe me,
Onalee."

I groaned. "You'd better start at the
beginning and don't leave out any details
this time."

"Okay," she said, twisting her hands.
She paused, took a shuddering breath, and
began. "After you, like, told us about Roy,
Pete started driving by Pembower's house to
check on him, like, every day. He kept
getting madder and madder about it, you
know? He even, like, saw that jerk kick
Roy one day. He said he had to do
something. You had already tried calling

animal control and he did too. I guess
they've got too many other dogs and cats to
worry about. Anyway, nothing ever changed
for Roy.

"He talked about it, like, all the
time. So that day we were together and he
said, 'Tonight's the night.' I'm like, what
do you mean? He said, 'There's no moon out
tonight. I'm going to go over after
midnight and liberate Roy.' Seriously? I'm
thinking. But I said, 'I'm in.' He tried to
talk me out of it, but I made him take me.
Kinda dumb, huh?" She looked up at us with
a wry smile.

"Wow!" I was at a loss for words as I
tried to piece this together with what we
already knew. "What happened when you guys
went over there?"

"Roy heard us climbing over the fence
and started barking. Apparently Pembower
was still awake, saw us and came barreling
out the back door. He was screaming and
swearing. He's faster than he looks, and he
was on us in no time. He grabbed my arms
and threw me, and I landed against Roy's
dog house. I got the breath knocked out of
me, so I just laid there for a moment. That
made Pete go berserk, and he started
punching him, but Pembower was giving as

good as he got. As soon as I could, I got
to my feet and tried to pull Pete off.
Finally I got through to him, and we got
the heck out of there." She looked at us
again.

"Was Pembower okay when you left and
did you have Roy?"

"Yeah, Pembower was standing by Roy as
we climbed back over his fence and ran to
the car."

"But Pete wound up with Roy, right?"
Marti looked back and forth between Lacey
and me.

Lacey nodded. "Pete took me home. I
made him come in, and I checked him over.
He didn't seem to be hurt too badly, so I
patched him up rather than going to the ER.
He left my house about 2:00 a.m. and told
me he was going to turn in. I went to bed,
too."

Marti and I looked at her expectantly.
Lacey was again staring at the table. "Pete
and Roy?" prodded Marti.

Lacey swallowed and cleared her
throat. "I guess after Pete left my house,
he went back to Pembower's place. He says
he snuck in and Pembower didn't hear him
that time. He just grabbed Roy and left."

"Was Pembower alive then?" I asked.

"I don't know. Pete didn't see him."

"Lacey how do you know that Pete didn't get into it again with Pembower and wind up killing him?"

Lacey's face crumpled in anguish and her eyes brimmed with tears. "You guys, I really like him. I might even be in love with him. He can't be a murderer, can he?"

"He sure doesn't seem like it. I like him too," I said gently.

"So Pete's version of the story is that the last time he saw Pembower was with you?" Marti asked.

"Yes."

"Then, why did you get picked up for questioning?" She pressed.

"I don't know. When they didn't come after me right away, I thought I was, like, home free." She grimaced but I think it was actually a failed grin.

"Are you completely sure you haven't left out any little details this time? Say, like that you were armed with a baseball bat or something?"

Tears flowed again. "Onalee, I thought you were my friend. I thought you knew me better than that."

"Okay, but you've got to admit that you haven't been exactly on the up and up with me."

"I know. I'm sorry," she said in a small voice.

"How well do you really know Pete? You said yourself that he went berserk," Marti said.

"Yeah, but that was because he thought Pembower had hurt me," Lacey said, eyes, downcast. "Pete hates that kind of thing." She looked up at me, "But, I know he couldn't kill anybody."

***

"What do you think?" Marti asked as we left the jail.

"About Lacey? She's a lousy cook, but she's no killer."

"And Pete?"

"I guess I'm not as convinced about his innocence anymore. I don't like that 'berserk' business."

"Looks like it's time for the Gonzalez-O'Conner Operatives to get down to brass tacks," she pronounced as she high-stepped down the jailhouse stairs to the sidewalk.

G-O-O? You want to name our firm GOO?" I asked, sprinting after her.

Chapter Eighteen

We needed a plan. First we drove over to Lacey's apartment and rounded up Kitty to take to my house. Of course, that also meant carting food, dog dishes, a bed and some of her favorite toys. "We need to fill in some gaps, On." Marti piped up from the back seat. Lacey had warned us that Kitty would insist on riding in the front.

"Yeah, I know. Let's try to find out Pembower's ex-wife's address on the Internet. We might be able to track down his kids that way, too."

We turned into my drive. Kitty knew where she was and galloped up my steps to meet her beloved Dashiell. As the two best canine friends raced around the house, the two best human buddies fired up the computer. Meanwhile, I surfed the old fashioned way through the phone book. Gerald Pembower was listed, though no address was given. No other kin were in the book, at least under the Pembower name. We got nowhere with Google either.

"I guess we'll have to go over to the drycleaners and if she's working, do a stakeout, and follow her home.

"Ooh. Now you're talking," Marti said, eyes aglow.

"It's not—"

"What?"

"Nothing." *I should tell Ms. Potentate Gonzalez how truly boring staking out actually is.* "Marti, you ought to stay here. The stakeout could prove to be dangerous, and you're inexperienced in that phase of the business."

"On, I'm perfectly capable of conducting an undercover op. You should stay home and take care of Dashiell and Kitty."

"I'd never forgive myself if something happened to you and I was the one who'd sent you into harm's way." We were in the living room and Kitty and Dashiell's heads swung back and forth listening to this exchange.

"I can take care of myself," she insisted.

I heaved a sigh, "If there's nothing I can do to stop you, then, alright."

The four of us ate a quick lunch. I found one of my suits to drop off at

Hot Dog

Carthmore's, where Sharon Pembower worked.
We had no idea what her hours were, but we
had to start someplace. Hopefully the
workers would be wearing name tags.

"Yikes, On, it's really cooled off."
Marti said as we stepped out the door.

The sky had darkened, and the wind
came at us from the west at a pretty good
clip. I spun on my heel, unlocked the door,
and we changed from shorts and t-shirts
into jeans and long-sleeved shirts. We
grabbed our jackets and once again, set
off.

***

The woman at the counter looked up as we
came in. She seemed about the right age to
have been married to Pembower. Her brown
and gray hair hung limply around her
shoulders.

Marti made eye contact with me. I knew
what she was thinking. No name tag. Shoot
and double shoot! I placed the suit on the
counter. "I'd like to get this dry-cleaned.
Do you think you can get this stain out?" I
pointed at a mark.

"Do you know what it is?"

"Yup. It's chocolate."

"Figures," Marti said under her
breath.

A small smile passed over the woman's face. "We should be able to." She reached for a pad of paper. "Name?"

"Hi. I'm Onalee O'Conner. I should have introduced myself." I stuck my hand out.

Startled, she shook my hand. "Hello."

"This is my good friend Marti Gonzalez. She's visiting from Detroit."

Rising to the occasion, as always, Marti also shook hands. "Everyone is so friendly here. It's just great. I'm terrible with names. What did you say yours was again?"

"Sharon."

"Hi, Sharon," Marti said beaming at her.

Sharon turned to me. "I need a phone number for you, too."

I gave her my number and we scooted out the door. "That must be her, unless they have two Sharons on board." I said.

I dropped Marti at her car and she drove back to begin her vigil. Meanwhile, I planned to do some snooping around the Pembower neighborhood.

Marti had shown me the houses of the people she'd talked with. I planned to try the rest of them, but it was a weekday, so

I might have the same problem she had connecting with people. In fact, no one appeared to be home at the first two houses. I was on the porch of the third when a car pulled into the driveway. An elderly couple got out and approached me. "May we help you?" the woman asked warily.

"Um, hi. My name is Onalee O'Conner. Do you live here?"

"Yes."

"Could I ask you a few questions? It's about Gerald Pembower."

"Are you a policewoman?" the man asked.

"No. Some friends of mine have gotten kind of mixed-up in the whole thing and I promised them I'd see if I could find out anything."

"Mixed-up in it? Did they kill him?"

"No, but the police think they may have. Do you know anyone who might have done it?"

The man and woman exchanged a glance. "Why would the police think your friends had anything to do with the murder?" He asked, not letting go of it.

"They got into a fight with him that night." A bit of exasperation may have tinged my voice. *I wasn't supposed to be the one spilling my guts. What a bunch of nosy parkers!*

"Fight? Whatever did they fight about? Are you sure your friends didn't do it, honey?" *She is as bad as he is. Is this what I will turn into in forty years? Or, had I already?*

"They fought about Pembower's dog, Roy."

The woman nodded her head. "I see. What happened to that dog?"

"He's at the pound and being taken care of. Can you think of anyone who would kill Mr. Pembower?"

"We didn't know anything about it until we read about it in the papers. We were downstate visiting the kids."

"What about your neighbors? Are there any that you think I should talk to?"

"I imagine someone might be able to help you out." the man cut in as he unlocked the door. "It's been nice chatting with you." He turned to his wife, "Come on in the house before you catch your death of cold, Barbara."

"Did you have any problems with—" I was talking to a closed door. See if I ever call on them again! They were right about one thing, though, the mercury was dropping like a Petoskey stone. Shivering, I hustled back to my car, flicked on the ignition and turned the heat to high. The house next door to The Inquisitives belonged to the retired teacher. I decided to try the one next to her place, but not until my hands warmed up a little and my teeth quit chattering.

No one was home there, and at the next house in line they blew me off. I was moseying back down the street when I saw Mrs. Marsden, the teacher, out on her front stoop shaking out a rug. She hadn't given Marti any information, but at least she'd talked to her. And being an old lady, her house would probably be a bone-thawing 90 degrees.

* * *

"Goodbye Mrs. Marsden. Thank you so much for the lemon tea with dollops of rum. It was the perfect drink on a cold day." She closed the door, and I trotted to my car. Thankfully, we hadn't gotten into the hand baskets to hell discussion. Maybe there'd been more rum the day Marti talked with her. Or less? Instead we spoke of the old days around Petoskey before it became so trendy. I hadn't had her for a teacher since I'd gone to a different elementary school, but I'll bet she'd have been a good one.

We'd sat on her sofa, and she served tea out of an ornate tea pot into delicate china cups and saucers. I didn't slight my sleuthing duties entirely; we'd discussed her neighbor Mr. Pembower. "Where did he work?" I'd asked.

"He didn't. At least not for the last few years."

"Really? I would have guessed that he was in his mid-fifties. That's kind of young for retirement."

"He was in an accident. An elderly man ran a stop sign and smashed into his car on the driver's side. Gerald was hurt quite badly. His legs were shattered and his back was broken in a number of places. He hired one of those lawyers you see on television all the time. Do you know whom I mean, Onalee?" She took a sip of her tea.

"Harry Cotton or someone like that?"

"Exactly. They got every last penny that old man had. He even had to sell his house to pay Mr. Pembower and his lawyer off." Mrs. Marsden shook her head sadly.

"Wow. That's a shame. Of course, if Pembower couldn't work anymore—"

Hot Dog

"I know. There are always two sides to everything, aren't there, dear?" She looked over at me. "Let me freshen up your tea, sweetie." She poured more tea and then a second helping of rum. I now felt quite toasty.

Mrs. Marsden told me that the old man who maimed Pembower, Raymond Rudolph, was still alive. She had been in school with him, Class of '48. It seemed that he had a strong motive for murder but to be honest, I didn't know of many octogenarian evildoers.

I wanted to discuss these revelations with Marti, but she was probably still on stakeout. If I went over to her, I knew she'd rope me into finishing off her tour of duty. *My best bet was to stay clear of Ms. G. As I always say, "Inaccessibility is the mother of freedom."*

Chapter Nineteen

I circled back to my house. It was time for Dashiell and Kitty's outing and, sadly, time to put away my fall jacket and slip on a winter parka. I paused a moment and sent best wishes into the universe for Marti to be blessed with a good heater in her stakeout-mobile. It was the least I could do.

After our sojourn I turned again to my primitive search engine, the phone book. At 86 years of age, I doubted whether Raymond Rudolph had given up his landline in favor of a cell phone. It turned out that he hadn't, and his address was across town on Carriage Lane. He probably lived in the senior citizens' low income apartments. It was 3:30, just enough time to fit in a chat with Mr. Rudolph. Keeping in mind my commitment to un-reachability, I left my cell phone on the kitchen table.

Skipping down the steps, I got a face-full of the wind hurtling down at us from the north. I now had my winter jacket and gloves on but could have used a wool hat as well. I jumped in the car. As I motored along the highway towards Carriage Lane, I caught glimpses of the bay, erupting in wild, white-capped glory. Also, I kept an eye out for the homeless man, Ron, who Mustang-Michael had told me frequented the bike path between town and the county park.

I thought of poor Marti, huddled over her steering wheel, hour after endless hour, and nearly veered in the direction of Carthmore's. But no, I must allow her to successfully carry out her mission. I pushed on to Carriage Lane.

At the locked front door of the building were rows of buzzers next to apartment numbers without names. No one was around to let me in. I pushed one at random and waited for the length of time I estimated it would take someone to traverse twenty or so feet with a walker. There was no response. I tried another buzzer and waited once more the requisite walker-traverse time, again to no avail. I peered into the glass beside the door as a diminutive lady on the other side looked up at me. She opened the door.

"I'll bet you forgot the room number of the person you came to see," she said with a giggle.

"Thanks. Actually, I did." I said straying to the disingenuous side of the ledger. "His name is Raymond Rudolph. You don't know which apartment he lives in, do you?"

"Ray? I don't know the room number but I know where it is. Follow me."

We took an elevator up to the second floor and slowly but steadily made our way down a corridor. The hallway was empty but I could hear the sound of television sets and smell cooking odors. Whatever was being prepared made my mouth water. My guide, Mildred, stopped in front of an open door and called in, "Ray, I've brought you some company."

A tall thin fellow stepped into his living room and then hurried out to meet us. "Hello, Mildred. You're just in time for some homemade bread." He inspected me and stuck his hand out, smiling. "I don't believe we've met. I'm Ray Rudolph."

I introduced myself as we shook hands.

"Why don't you two girls come on in here and tell me if this batch is any good." As we entered his apartment and took chairs at his dining table, he walked back to his kitchen and returned a minute or so later with a large loaf of golden-crusted bread. He placed it on the table in front of us along with plates, knives, napkins, a stick of butter and pot of jam.

"Jam's made from last season's rhubarb," he said and began slicing the bread with a large cleaver.

Mildred and I each helped ourselves to a thick hunk of the bread. I slathered mine with jam while Mildred chose the butter. Biting into the warm, crusty slice of paradise on a plate, I whimpered with satisfaction. Mewing noises issued from Mildred as she experienced her first bite.

Ray grinned at our reaction. "Guess I finally perfected my formula. Now, to what do I owe this pleasure, Miss O'Conner?"

I hated to bring up the unfortunate past, especially after he'd been such a gracious host to a stranger. "I, um, I was talking with Mrs. Marsden earlier today."

"My old classmate. How is Helen?"

"She's fine." I took a breath and dove in, "I'd been speaking with her because we're looking into the Pembower murder and she— Mr. Rudolph swallowed and looked away.

He turned back, "Yes. Go on."

"She told me about the accident and,"
"The lawsuit?"

"Um, yes." Mildred quit eating and sat staring at her plate.

"That was a very sad chapter for both of us," he paused and shook his head. "I ruined that poor man's life. It's true that I lost my house and all of my retirement savings," he looked straight at me. "But I didn't have to lie around in bed for months on end and lose the ability to earn a living. Does that answer your question?"

Mildred looked at me reproachfully. "I'm sorry to bring it up," I said. "You've been so nice, offering me this fabulous bread and jam."

"That's okay. The police stopped by after he was killed, and they also had questions. I imagine I'm thought to have a motive. But that's pretty far from the truth, since not a day goes by that I don't wish things had turned out differently."

"Can I ask what happened?" I said as Mildred glared at me.

"It's no secret. I was driving home. In those days I lived over off Landau Avenue. I was listening to a book on tape. Now I guess they'd say I was driving distracted. I never noticed that the light at the intersection of Mitchell and Landau was red. I drove right through it and

collided with Mr. Pembower. I was bruised
up a bit but my engine protected me. They
had to use the Jaws of Life to extract him.
Long story short, he got a lawyer and sued
me."

"That's scary. I think it could happen
to anybody. We're all distracted at times."

"It's nice of you to say that. But
what if he'd died that day? I don't know if
I could have lived with it." His face was
grim.

"Did you know him?"

"Not really. I saw him a few times
during the process of the legal
proceedings, but we never really talked. I
guess I figured if I got to know him, I'd
feel even worse."

"Maybe, but he wasn't the nicest guy
in the world."

"Other people have mentioned that, but
nobody deserves to be maimed like that."

"It was an accident, Ray." Mildred
hissed.

"Can I ask what the settlement was?"

Mildred shook her finger as she
scolded, "Young lady, where are your
manners? I shouldn't have let you in the
door."

"It's okay," he said mildly. "I have no secrets. It was $1,500,000. They asked for two million and my insurance company's lawyers negotiated it down to that amount. Yes, it's a lot of money, but not considering what he lost."

I consider myself a good judge of character. Then again, I've never known anyone who didn't see themselves that way. But as sure as my name is Onalee O'Conner, this sweet man couldn't be a murderer. "Thank you for answering all of my questions and for your hospitality, Mr. Rudolph. I think I'd better get out of your hair now."

I found my own way back to the front entrance of the building. Maybe it was time to check on poor Marti. Driving over to Carthmore's, I saw no sign of the Martmobile anywhere. It was about 4:30, and storm clouds were turning our fall afternoon into an early twilight.

Chapter Twenty

Returning to the house, I found out that Marti was ensconced in a tubful of hot, soapy bubbles. Conversing through the bathroom door, she told me she'd persevered and followed Sharon Pembower to her apartment facility, and noted which unit she'd entered.

"Do you want to go over there tonight to talk with her?"

"I will if I'm out of the tub by then."

"You hungry?"

"Starved but not as hungry as I am cold."

"Zowie! Feel like Chinese or Thai? I could run over to the restaurant and get carryout."

"Perfect."

Over dinner Marti filled me in on her frigid vigil. If she'd removed all of the commentary related to boredom and frozen body parts, her story could have been summarized in a couple of sentences. As she put it, Hell, Michigan could jolly well freeze over before she went on another stakeout.

"Why didn't you turn the car on and get some heat?"

"I did, but I was there for hours and my gas gauge was almost on empty."

I told her about my adventures, but using discretion, left out the parts about hot toddies and homemade bread with jam.

By 7:00 we were on our way to Mrs. Pembower's place. We rang the doorbell of the unit Marti had written down. "One of the first rules of successful sleuthing, On," she'd informed me, "is to always carry a smart phone to jot down notes with, or in your case, a small pad of paper and a pen would work."

Mrs. Pembower came to the door and opened it just as far as the security chain allowed. "Yes? Can I help you?" She looked puzzled.

"Hello again, Sharon. We met you today at the Laundromat," I said.

"Yes, I remember," she said slowly, unlatching the chain and stepping out onto the porch.

"Could we ask you some questions about your husband?"

"Monty? What kind of questions? What's this about?" she asked warily.

"I guess it would be your former husband then. We're looking into his murder."

"Who are you again?"

We introduced ourselves. "One of our friends is a suspect in the crime and we're trying to help her out by getting to the bottom of it."

"I don't know what use I'll be to you. We divorced four years ago."

"After his accident?"

She smiled sadly. "No. As they say, if I didn't have bad luck, I wouldn't have any luck at all. We divorced and split what few assets there were. About a month later he was in the accident and got a boat load of money." She looked away, "If I'd only known."

She wrapped her arms around her body. We had to make our move or she was going to scamper back into her warm abode. "Could we just have a few minutes of your time, Mrs.—"

"Mrs. Stuart. Sharon Stuart."

Marti flashed her a dimpled grin. "Please? You won't believe the day I've had. I sat in my freezing cold car all day waiting until you left work so I could find out where you live. I couldn't drink coffee to keep warm or I'd have to go to the bathroom all the time. You have no idea how I suffered. Please don't make me think that was all just a waste."

A small smile flitted across Sharon's face. "All right. Come in." Amazing. Marti used the truth to get ahead. I'd have to remember that technique.

The front door opened up directly into the living room. Mrs. Stuart went over to an easy chair and sat down. Marti and I stood in the doorway, still in our jackets. Marti looked at me and shrugged then we both unzipped our jackets and laid them on the arm of a nearby chair. We walked over and took seats on the couch, facing her. "Your husband, is it Monty? He's not here tonight?" I asked, to get a conversation going.

"No. He works afternoons at Randlemann's Manufacturing."

"In the Little Traverse Industrial Park?"

She looked over at me, her glasses reflecting the light and masking her eyes. "That's the one."

"How'd you two meet?" Marti asked.

Hot Dog

She smiled, remembering. "He was a customer, and a real looker, too. He'd drop his clothes off and we'd wash them for him. It's one of the services we offer," she said in an aside to me then faced Marti again. "One day, after my divorce was finalized he come strollin' in as usual. Only this time he kinda took stock of me, I guess you'd say. He said, 'You sure look like someone who could use a friend.'

I must have been looking down because I looked up into the kindest eyes I ever seen. We gabbed for a bit and I probably charged him for the laundry though I don't remember doing it. Then he asked if I wanted to have a drink with him. Imagine! Me goin' out with the best lookin' guy in the county." She shook her head, her face glowing.

"Did you say yes?" I asked.

"Of course."

"And now you two are married. That's wonderful. How long?" Marti asked.

"It's coming on to our second anniversary."

"Was your ex upset?" I asked. "He never remarried, did he?"

Her face shut down again. "Who'd marry that low life? Everybody knew what a toad he was."

"Do you have kids?" Marti asked.

"I have a son and daughter."

"That's nice," I said. "Do they live around here?"

"Not really. Mandy lives in them apartments for poor people over by Walmarts and Junior is clear out in Conway.

"Did you and Gerald keep in touch?" Marti asked.

"Not if I could help it," she said with a shake of her head.

"When was the last time you saw him?" I asked.

She flicked her wrist to check the time but answered. "Garsh, I guess it was a couple of weeks before he was killed. He brought his clothes over to the shop sometimes for us to wash. I imagine it was when he picked them up. Anywho," she said, getting up. "I work early tomorrow and I still got some chores to finish before my Monty gets home."

Marti leaped to her feet. "Of course. Thank you so much for helping us out," she smiled at her. "Do you think it would be okay to talk with your son and daughter?"

Hot Dog

Sharon frowned and looked away from us. "I suppose you could stop in and see Mandy, but she's a busy girl what with her son and all. Gerald Junior? I don't know."

"Let me write their addresses down so that we don't have to bother you again."

That Marti is a smooth one. I guess she can teach me a few techniques, after all.

Sharon frowned again as she deliberated then she caved in to the Gonzalez charm. Marti took down the addresses and phone numbers, we snagged our jackets, opened Sharon's front door, stepped out and into a blizzard.

"Onalee!" Marti shouted to be heard over the wind. "You've got to be kidding me. We were in shorts and tee shirts on the beach this morning."

The wind tore a chuckle from my lips.

Chapter Twenty-One

We maneuvered carefully over slick roads as snow eddied around the car. Scampering up my steps, we opened the door and were nearly bowled over by dog power. Both Dashiell and Kitty leaped and circled in an ecstatic welcome.

"Poodle Boy, how are you? Kitty, hello girl." I said as we petted heads and backs while they whirled around our legs. "Marti, I need to take these critters out for a quick jaunt. Why don't you stay here and get out of your wet shoes. I won't be long." I slipped out of my own soggy footwear and dug my winter boots out of the closet.

After snapping on the leashes we bolted out the door. Dashiell and Kitty kicked up their heels and pranced down the street. We hadn't gone far before Dashiell threw himself on his back and thrashed around in the snow. Kitty rushed over to him, growling, and they wrestled, rolling over and over. I dropped both of the leashes and jumped out of the way of the thrashing bodies. They both finally rolled to their stomachs, panting and grinning at each other.

I got hold of the leashes again and urged them to their feet. We proceeded around the block and back to the house. Marti, in her pj's and a robe, was curled up under a throw on the couch. I unleashed the dogs, and went into the garage for firewood. My first armload was logs and cardboard. Next, I sorted through the kindling I'd gathered the previous summer, selected a number of sticks and then picked up some old newspapers. I piled it all by the hearth.

Marti switched to a chair nearer the wood stove and watched as I balled up the papers and laid the kindling and cardboard in the stove. I put a small log in and then lit the papers with my grill lighter. Flames roared to life. I sat in the other fireside chair and we watched as the fire devoured the paper then licked into cardboard and kindling. Waves of heat radiated out of the little stove pressing comfort and contentment upon us.

"This is nice, On," Marti sighed. We watched the flames without much conversation. Eventually, I talked myself

into leaving the circle of heat long enough
to pj-up and grab my paperback. Soon after
I'd settled back in my chair, the doorbell
rang. "Who'd be out on a night like
tonight?" I asked through a chorus of
canine commentary.

Marti answered with a shrug. I wrapped
my robe tighter around me and went to the
door. Lacey, in shorts and a short-sleeved
shirt, was on my porch, hopping from foot
to foot. As soon as I opened the door she
charged in. Kitty lunged for her, barking
excitedly with Dash on her heels.

*What do you say to somebody who has
just been released from jail? Are
congratulations in order?* Not knowing, I
stepped in between the two dogs and hugged
her, saying nothing.

Clinging to me, she said, "This has,
seriously, been one of the worst days of my
life."

"Come sit by the fire," I said,
leading her into the living room.

She stood right in front of the
woodstove. After a few minutes she stopped
shaking and turned to us. "Thank you so
much for taking care of Kitty." The dog,
who hadn't left Lacey's side, gazed up at
her.

"Of course. It was a treat for Dashiell." I paused. "Lacey, did you find out anything more about the murder?"

She shivered again. "No, that place was awful. They kept asking me the same questions, over and over again. I'm sure they didn't believe a word I said, and they didn't tell me anything."

"You must be starved. Let me get you some dinner."

After Lacey had eaten two helpings of soup, she said she was going directly home to take a long, hot shower. I loaned her a sweatshirt, sweatpants, and a jacket to wear and she and Kitty left.

Afterwards, Marti and I sat back down by the fire. I think both of us wondered why we hadn't filled Lacey in on the intel we'd gathered that day. I still didn't think she was capable of murder, but . . .

Chapter Twenty-Two

The following day we woke to forty degrees
and sunshine. The snow was melting, but
Bootless-Marti Gonzalez wisely opted out of
the dog walking session. Dashiell and I
strolled along a deserted beach as waves
roared in from yesterday's winds. I walked
along, lost in thought about the previous
day's events.

As we made our way back home, we met a
dog and a human. The dogs' tails wiped the
air as they gamboled towards each other.
The two sniffed as I gushed about the other
dog's looks. He was gorgeous, possibly even
in the same league as Dashiell. We took
them both off their leashes and they
played. The human was an attractive young
lady in her early twenties. I introduced
the D-Dog and myself.

"I'm Piper, and that's Reggie," she
said with a smile.

Piper? Hmmmm. They wrestled a while
longer and then Dashiell and I tromped on
through the puddles towards home. *It struck
me, and not for the first time, the*

significant extent of the generational name
shift. Dogs now have human names like
Reggie and Dashiell, while people are
called erstwhile dog names such as Brandy,
Cheyenne, and of course Piper. I'm just
waiting for some kid to come along named
Chopper or Fido.

Back at the house, Marti was catching
up on emails. I made another call to the
dog pound to see how Roy was doing. No one
had claimed him, and his time was running
out. Marti finished, and I hopped on the
computer to check my correspondence. There
were two bid requests for appraisal jobs,
neither of which looked very enticing.
Maybe I should open a private eye agency. I
couldn't speak for Stakeout Girl, but for
me, yesterday had been an interesting and
event-filled day. Much more exciting than
spending my time trying to come up with a
value for a pole barn in downtown Podunk
Center.

For lunch, we heated some steel-cut
oats I had cooked a few days ago. Over our
meal, we decided to drop in on the two
Pembower offspring. We discussed what
questions we most wanted answered from
them, assuming they would talk to us.

Connie Doherty

From what Sharon said, it sounded like our best shot was with the daughter, Mandy. We didn't know where she worked, if at all, so she could be home in the middle of the day. We'd try her first and if we struck out there, we'd try Pembower, Junior.

Although we had Mandy's address, it took a bit of backing and forthing down various drives in her apartment complex before we came upon the right building. In each structure there were four doorways that opened to interior hallways leading to the apartments. Mandy's apartment was on the second floor. We rang the doorbell three or four times, but no one answered. Sticking to our plan, we hopped in my car, drove back through town and then north a few miles to Conway.

Junior lived on a street several blocks from the highway on the outskirts of town. No car was in the driveway, and the house was dark inside. Not surprisingly, no one came to the door.

I checked my watch. It was a little before two o'clock. I turned to Marti, "What do you think?"

"We talked about calling on Sharon's husband, Monty. Why don't we do that?"

Hot Dog

"Capital idea," I said as we walked back toward my car.

It didn't take us more than a few minutes to reach Petoskey. "Maybe we should wait a little before we go to Monty's place. He may still be sleeping, if he works the afternoon shift. I think that's usually until 12:00 or 1:00 in the morning." We decided to drop by my house and take Dashiell for an early walk. After that, it was nearly 3:00 and probably a good time to catch him.

He came to the door after one ring of the buzzer. Just as Sharon had said, he was an attractive guy. He stood about six feet tall, towering over Marti and me, and looked very fit. He stepped aside, inviting us into the apartment.

As we told him our purpose, frown lines formed between his eyes. "I'm not sure I can help you much. I tried to stay as far away from that poor excuse of a human being as I could." Sitting down, he gestured towards the couch. "You ladies please take a seat."

"Do you have any idea who might have wanted him dead?" I asked, sitting in the same spot I had taken last night.

He chuckled and his eyes crinkled into
well-worn laugh lines. "I guess you could
fill a football stadium with that guy's
enemies." He looked at the floor and then
up at us. "I'd be in there with the rest of
them. I didn't know him until I married
Sharon, but the things she told me—" he
shook his head.

"He was abusive?" I asked.

He turned to me, "Oh yeah. Always
putting her down, too, you know?"

"I had a few run ins with him myself,"
I said.

"Then you know what he was like."

"When was the last time you saw him?"
asked Marti.

He stroked his chin as he thought.
"Boy, I guess it was when we ran into him
at the grocery store. He was as ugly as he
could be to Sharon. I don't get it. A nice
person like her. Why did he think he had to
treat her like dirt?"

I shook my head. "It's not even
comprehensible to normal people, I guess.
What did he do that day?"

"I don't remember for sure. The usual
stuff, I guess. Insults. Sneering at her. I
just remember feeling like I'd like to deck
him."

"Did you two ever get into it?"

"Naw. Guys like that don't ever pick on anyone their own size."

"You're right. He was definitely a bully. Do you know his kids very well?"

"Junior and Mandy? We see them once in a while."

"What are they like?"

"They've got their problems, just like the rest of us."

"How'd they get along with their dad?" Marti asked.

"I only know what I've heard. I don't think Junior had much to do with his pop, but Mandy and him were close."

"Even though her dad was so mean?" I asked. "How could anyone who knew that man like him?"

He shrugged. "He was her dad. Maybe he treated her better."

"Do you think it was because of the inheritance?" I asked.

"You mean she was shining up to him so that she didn't get cut out?" I nodded. "Naw, she was his good buddy before that, from what Shar tells me. Now, you ladies will have to excuse me, I've got to get ready for work." He got to his feet.

Marti and I rose as well. "Is there anything you can think of that we should know or anyone else we could talk to?" I asked.

"I'd be surprised if you get anywhere with those two kids. Let's see, Shar mentioned one time . . . who was that? We ran into him at the Flywheeler's show last summer. Yeah, she said he was a friend of Pembower's. You could've blown me over with a feather. I honestly didn't think he had any friends. Anyhow, I think he used to work with the guy." He walked towards the front door with Marti and me lagging behind.

"Where did he work?"

Monty smiled as he opened the door. "You two are harder to get rid of than some of those door to door Bible thumpers. He worked at Dobbs and Merrick Brothers Construction. I'm shutting the door now."

"Thank you so much," I said and Marti grinned at him.

Chapter Twenty-Three

We drove back toward my place. "I'm glad that poor Sharon has a decent husband now."

"Me too. On, why don't we swing by Pembower's house? Maybe if we look things over again, we'll get some inspiration."

I turned off the highway and on to the side street running by his house. I drove slowly along his backyard fence where it all began that day with Brownie/Roy.

"Let's park the car and survey the scene."

"All righty," I swerved into the parking lane beside the curb.

We sat there a while in silence, then Marti, our self-appointed lead investigator, began to summarize all that we knew so far. It didn't take long.

She ticked our results off using her fingers, "We've interviewed a few of the neighbors, his ex-wife, her new husband and I guess you could say, Lacey since we've talked to her about it."

"Also, I interviewed the guy he sued, Raymond Rudolph and the homeless guy in the

Mustang," I said to get credit where credit was most assuredly due.

"Honestly, I think we're a long way from cracking this case. If the son and daughter don't talk to us, we'll basically have zip," she said dispiritedly. Then, perking up, she said, "Come on, let's go reconnoiter the house," and opened the car door.

"Marti. People will see us and call the cops."

"You're friends with all of them, so if we do get caught, which we won't, they'll let us off."

She was out the door. *Why do so many of my friends come from the lunatic fringe?* I climbed out and trailed after her. It was a bungalow-style house, so there were probably two bedrooms down and one large bedroom upstairs. Marti was at the large front window. She cupped her hands around her eyes then turned back to me, "I can't see anything. It looks like he's got a shade covering the whole window."

We tried the windows on all four sides of the house, but the view was the same.

She caught me glancing over my shoulder. "Relax, no one is watching us.

Remember, everyone around here works during the day."

"We've left footprints in the mud around all the windows." I said. "People will be able to see that someone was at the crime scene."

"Let's check out the garage. Maybe we can even get into it."

The Pembower garage was detached and situated on the side street. Marti tried to open the overhead door, but it appeared to be locked. There was a small entry door on the side and she tried her luck with that one as well, but to no avail. Near the door was a window, and again she attempted to look inside. Given my prudent nature, I hung back and watched.

"I can see some kind of big truck. I think it's dark colored." She pushed at the window sash, and it slid up. Swiveling her head she shot me a meaningful glance. "I'm going in."

"Marti, no." I looked around again. The street seemed empty, but who knew how many prying eyes lurked behind window curtains. She hoisted one leg over the sill, pushed herself up and over.

"What do you see?" I asked Ms. Sub Rosa.

"I'm trying to find a light switch. Come on in, it's easy."

"They may have shut the electricity off," I said as a light came on giving me an eyeful. That did it. I clambered over the window sill and into the garage. There was a lawn mower along with various gardening tools, but it was the big black truck with tinted windows that sent my heart racing. I scurried around to the rear of the vehicle and found the bumper sticker with "Don't Tread on Me"

"Oh my gosh, Marti. This truck used to be by the bike path a lot of mornings. And, get this, the guy who owned this truck is the one who was hassling the scary looking homeless guy."

Marti looked puzzled. "What?"

"Maybe I didn't tell you about that. Michael, the homeless man in the Mustang told me about it. This means the scary-looking homeless guy did know Pembower. Maybe he did kill him."

"It sure gives him a motive."

We looked inside the truck and around the garage but didn't find anything else that seemed noteworthy. Turning off the light, we climbed back out the window. As soon as my feet hit the ground, I was

moving toward the car. My roving eyes
didn't find anyone watching us or anything
untoward. Marti trotted after me.

Reaching the vehicle, I slid into the
seat, turned the ignition and put it in
drive as Marti's door slammed. "Wait, On, I
don't have my seat belt fastened," she
grumbled.

I stepped on the brake, "My goodness
you're a poky one."

The seat belt clicked and I stepped on
the accelerator. We motored down an empty
road. A car turned on to our street a block
or so behind us but moved up on us rather
swiftly. Suddenly, there were flashing
lights and a siren. "Gnats."

Chapter Twenty-Four

"How fast were you going?" Marti asked as I maneuvered to the curb.

"The speed limit is 25 miles per hour and I was going about 28. This is harassment, plain and simple."

Mr. Costas himself strode up to my car. I lowered the window. "Good afternoon, Camille," I said with a toothy grin.

"Ms. O'Conner." He bent his head to look in the window. "Miss Gonzalez." He nodded at her then turned to me. "Do you know why I stopped you?"

"I imagine it was for driving three miles over the speed limit. Sorry. I was blowing the carbon out."

"Very funny. You were clocked at over the posted speed. However, there's another matter I wish to discuss with you. One of the residents of this neighborhood reported seeing someone or some ones skulking around the home of Gerald Pembower. Given your keen skills as an amateur sleuth, I thought perhaps you may have noticed something out of order in your travels."

Hot Dog

"Golly, no, I didn't. Marti, did you see anything suspicious?"

Costas turned his narrowed eyes on her.

"No, but we'll certainly watch from now on, Detective. It's wonderful seeing you again." she added.

"Miss Gonzalez, don't let your friend lead you astray."

My jaw dropped as the injustice of Costas' remarks slammed into me.

"Now, Ms O'Conner, I'll need to see your proof of insurance, driver's license and registration."

With a smug smile he wrote me up for speeding. At least he didn't take us over to Pembower's house where certain muddy footprints would have told a tale of two sleuths.

***

I glanced at my watch. It was a little before four o'clock. Making a snap decision, I swung the car around and we headed back into town.

"Where are we going now?"

"I haven't been to see Roy yet, and I miss him."

She frowned, "Roy? You mean the dog?"

Connie Doherty

"Yes. The pound is just on the other side of town, and I'm pretty sure they're open until 5:00." I knew if Marti could just see Roy and spend some time with him, she'd fall in love and adopt him. His life would be spared, and my pal Marti would have a wonderful companion.

A few minutes later we pulled up outside a grey, cement block, one-story building. We entered through a standard, commercial grade glass and metal door and found ourselves in a small reception area. The woman seated behind a large desk looked up and smiled. A placard on her desk announced her name as Ruth.

"Hello. May I help you?"

I thought her voice sounded like the lady I'd talked to when I'd made my calls to check on Roy. "Hi, Ruth?" She nodded. "My name is Onalee O'Conner and I think I've spoken with you before about the dog named Roy. Could we see him today?"

She frowned slightly. "I'm sorry. He's no longer with us."

Chapter Twenty-Five

My hands flew to my mouth as I sucked in some air. *He'd been snuffed out. Why hadn't Ruth warned me he was out of time when I'd called today?*

She rose to her feet. "No, you misunderstood. A man drove up here from downstate who has a dog rescue. He thinks he has someone interested in him."

My heartbeat slowed back to normal. Then again, I knew there were unscrupulous people who round up dogs for fighting and who knows what else. "When someone adopts a dog from here, is it like the rescues? Do you get information about them so that you know they're legit?"

Ruth opened her desk drawer and pulled out some business cards. Leafing through them, she found one and handed it to me. "This is the person who came for Roy. I'd spoken with him on the phone a couple of times and he came highly recommended by a local man who sometimes takes our dogs to find homes for them. I know he doesn't mind my passing along his information."

Connie Doherty

I studied the card and Marti read over my shoulder.

Dan Carlisle
Big Hearted Rescue
We specialize in Rotts, Pitts,
Pit-mixes and
German shepherd dogs.

I looked at Ruth. "This local man you mentioned, was it by any chance a fellow named Pete?"

"Oh, you know him? The pit bull king?"

"Yes, I do. And, he did say that he had a friend coming up from downstate to take Roy away."

"I've worked with Pete before, and if he gives his stamp of approval, it's good enough for me. Although," she cut her eyes at me, "as a dog lover myself, I looked Mr. Carlisle up on the computer and made a few phone calls. He checked out."

"Mind if I keep this card?"

She shook her head. "I may need it for future reference, but go ahead and copy the information down." She handed me a pen and pad of paper from her desk.

I jotted down the telephone numbers, web address, name of the rescue and the man's name. Turning to Marti, I said,

Hot Dog

"Since Roy is unavailable, do you want to look at some of the other dogs in the back?"

"I get it now," she said her eyes narrowing. "You wanted me to meet Roy and adopt him, didn't you?"

"You'd have loved him, Marti. It would have been great for both of you."

"You know for sure that Roy would get along with Frank's dog, Caesar?"

"I would certainly think so. He's a very sweet natured boy. Besides, you two aren't married yet."

She let out an audible sigh then turned to Ruth and thanked her for her time.

On the way home we stopped for Middle Eastern carry- out for dinner. Marti settled on a gyro and I got a falafel sandwich.

Later that evening, Mitch called and asked me to go with him to a foreign film playing at the library on Friday night. I'd been to their film theater before, and it was a nice community event. He said he'd pick me up, and we'd have dinner in downtown Petoskey then walk over to the library for the movie.

The following day I started work on an industrial building. After walking Dash down the windswept beach, I drove down to Gaylord to inspect the property. Frank called Marti with the news that he was back in town and wanted to see her as soon as possible. They were going out to lunch.

On the drive to Gaylord, I couldn't help but speculate if maybe today she would get a ring from him. I wondered if she'd move up here after they got married.

The manufacturing building was top notch. Although at 7,000 square feet it was somewhat small, it was a perfect sized building for northern Michigan. It was all dolled up with epoxy floors, infrared heaters and high intensity lighting in the shop; and updated offices. It had been put on the market and was under a purchase agreement within a month. A local business was expanding and had snapped it up.

It was so nice to be part of success stories again because of the robust economy. During the last deep recession, we appraisers had begun to feel like ghouls, being called in to sift through the bones of vacant and foreclosed buildings and record their spiral downward into price levels of decades gone by. Meanwhile, many of their owners faced financial ruin.

I inspected the property, drove around the neighborhood, and looked at seven other buildings in the area that had either recently sold or were listed for sale. By mid-afternoon, I finished up and motored back toward Petoskey.

As I crested the last hill overlooking my city, I saw heavy fog swirling around. All of the cars in the opposite lanes had their lights on. As I descended into the thick whiteness, I switched my bulbs on. Inching along through the fog, my thoughts turned inevitably to food and turned off for a quick stop at one of my favorite grocery stores.

As soon as I stepped inside the house, Dash rushed over and jumped on me, barking excitedly. "Mr. Dash. How are things in dog world? Yes, I missed you, too, my good fellow," I said as I petted him. It was similar to most conversations we had anytime I arrived home, even if I'd only been gone for a few minutes. "Dash, I know you want to go for a spin (I couldn't use the word w-a-l-k without unleashing his pre-walk euphoria) but can I take a couple of minutes first?"

Connie Doherty

I shrugged off my jacket and went to the kitchen. Quickly, I poured split peas into a strainer and washed them. Then I dumped them in a kettle with water and turned the burner on high.

I carefully measured out water at a temperature that yeast would enjoy and filled my measuring cup with the liquid and some sugar. The yeast was dumped into this mixture. Next, I pulled out my yellow bowl and added flour and salt, whisking to mix it up. I checked the yeast water. Small bubbles were rising to the top, telling me it was springing into action. The peas were boiling, so I turned off the burner. Their job was to soak for an hour and plump up.

Turning back to the yeasty concoction, I saw that the foaming had intensified. I mixed it into the flour, added a bit more water and stirred. I plunged my hands in and began turning it and kneading until it morphed into a smoothly cohesive ball of dough. I placed a clean kitchen towel over the top of the bowl and set it in the oven. The pilot light would provide the warmth needed for the bread to rise.

Dash was lying down just outside the kitchen, and following my movements with his eyes. As I walked out of the kitchen, he clambered to his feet and stared at me.

"Want to go for a walk?"

He danced to the door.

As we made our way to the beach, I noticed that the bank of fog had thickened. Visibility was reduced to about two hundred yards. Dash loped along the water's edge and disappeared into cottony air. Moments later, he burst through the opalescent curtain and ran to my side, droplets of moisture clinging to his black curls. I found a stick and threw it for him. We were in our own small white world between the pewter grey lake and silent dunes.

Returning home, I saw Marti's car in the drive. Dash saw it too and scampered up the porch stairs. I opened the door for him and unsnapped his leash. He bolted inside, thrilled she was back.

"We're home," I called out. There was no answer. Dash ran from room to room. This was odd. In the kitchen, I found a note from Marti saying that she'd gone for a walk. By the time she gets back out of the cold and damp, I thought, she'll welcome piping hot pea soup and freshly baked bread.

Connie Doherty

After turning my kettle of peas back on, I cut thin shavings of carrots and celery, and threw them in the soup. Then I peeled and diced potatoes and onions. A check of my bowl revealed that the bread had risen to about twice its size. I punched it down and formed it into long, thin loaves on a cookie sheet. Stirring the soup a bit, I turned the burner down to simmer.

Still no sign of Marti, so I switched on the computer and started searching for more industrial sales around the area. I was knee deep in the appraisal when the front door quietly opened. Dash leaped off his bed and skittered around the couch to meet Marti as she stepped inside. One look at her told me something was drastically wrong.

"What is it, Sweetie?"

She shook her head. "Frank kind of broke up with me." Dash eyed Marti but hung back and didn't jump on her. She petted him distractedly.

I strode over to give her a hug but she backed away.

"I'm soaking wet. Wait until I get my jacket off. Then a hug would feel great."

Hot Dog

"I'm so, so sorry," I said as she hung her wet coat by a register to dry. "But, 'kind of' broke up?"

"Yeah. He'd been head over heels in love with a woman years ago, but she moved away and broke his heart. Now, she's back in town and called him. He said he didn't want to lose me but that he had to see if he still felt the same about her."

"He wants to string you along until he decides between the two of you?" I asked, my hackles rising. I liked the guy but he was doing my friend wrong.

"No, he's not like that. We talked it through and he's going to start seeing her. He says it's something he has to do. Otherwise, he'll always wonder if she was the one for him." She sighed. "Meanwhile, it's over between us. He said if it didn't work out with Pamela, then he'd do his best to win me back, so we're going our separate ways for now."

She looked at me. "I suppose I could've talked him into seeing both of us at the same time, but I just couldn't. It would've driven me crazy, wondering all the time where he was and what he was doing."

"No, I think you did the right thing. I just never expected something like this."

Connie Doherty

"You and me both."

"You're shivering. Why don't you go in
and take a long, steamy bubble bath. I'll
run over to the grocery store and pick us
up a couple of gallons of cheap wine." I
was rewarded with a slight smile.

Two hours later, Marti and I were
seated at the kitchen table. I was
finishing my second bowl of soup in between
bites of the crusty baguettes. Marti ladled
out a small dollop of soup for herself, and
toyed with it as, God help me, I guzzled
mine down. Although I felt immense sorrow
for my friend, it didn't seem to adversely
affect my ever-ready appetite. If I'd only
known about this turn of events earlier, I
wouldn't have cooked one of my cold-and-
wet-autumn-evening favorite meals.

The wine and hot bath had taken the
chill out of Marti's bones, but they had
not cheered her. From experience, I knew
that only time would bring her back to her
usual, chipper self. I kept up a running
discussion about appraising, adventures
with Dash and everything else I could think
of. She listened to the conversational
deluge in a desultory way, adding a
noncommittal comment at times. After dinner
I asked if she'd like to discuss the case.

Hot Dog

"I'm beat. I think I'm going to turn in."

It was seven o'clock. She pushed the air bed to the middle of the floor and tested it for firmness. Turning to me, she said, "If you want to build a fire or watch TV, go ahead, it won't bother me."

The television would be about six feet from her bed.

"Um no, I'd just as soon read, though I will have to come through here to take Dashiell for a walk at about nine."

"I'll probably be sound to sleep by then," she said.

Chapter Twenty-Six

The following morning, Dash and I tiptoed around Marti, and went for our walk. A steady northwesterly wind tossed the trees around, and deep blue waves rushed against the shore. Near the water, Lacey was throwing sticks for Kitty to chase.

We began our sojourn towards the main beach. Lacey seemed a little subdued but otherwise back to her old self. She said that Pete was again out and about, but that the police had told both him and her not to leave town.

I mentioned that Marti and I had been nosing around but hadn't come up with anything that could help their case. Then I told her about Marti and Frank.

"No! She's seriously in love with him. I could tell," Lacey said.

"Maybe it'll all work out."

We walked along, both absorbed in our own thoughts until a splash in the lake caught our attention. A salmon had jumped and as we watched, leaped again into the air. Starting in August, salmon come into

shallow water, hunting for the streams of
their youth. Eventually, they try to make
their way up the rivers to spawn. At this
point, they are nearly at the end of their
lives. Today, we could see a couple of them
just off shore, circling as they searched.
Their fins crested the water like small
sharks.

As we watched the fish, Dashiell and
Kitty amused themselves by chasing seagulls
up and down the shore. Suddenly Dashielle
made an abrupt turn and loped behind a
beach shrub, with Kitty right behind him.
Uh oh.

We ran after them. Rounding the bush,
I found Dash flopped down on his back and
wriggling on a dead salmon. Kitty stood
nearby, possibly waiting her turn to have a
go at the delicious smelling detritus. I
leaped over to Dash and yanked him off the
fish. Eyes shining, he clambered to his
feet as I held him and clipped on his
leash. A wave of putrid fish smell poured
over me.

"Dash! Bad, bad, bad dog!" I yelled,
once again, breaking my vow to never become
a dog-yeller. "We're going home. Your walk
is over, young man." I stayed at the far
end of our six foot leash, but the air

around me was thick with the dead fish
miasma. Lacey had gotten hold of Kitty in
time, and the two of them walked behind us.

A few minutes later we left the beach.
"That was powerful stuff you got into, my
good fellow," I said as I shuffled along
the bike path. Dash was prancing, head and
tail held high. "Dash, like I always say,
there's more that separates our two species
than just the opposable thumbs." Just then,
I caught sight of Tommy hiding behind a
tree along the walkway. What an odd fellow
he is, I thought. The realization hit me
that he'd probably overheard my discussion
with the Dasher-Dog. Who was the crazy one
here?

As we entered the house, my plan was
to take Dash right to the bathtub. Marti
was still ensconced in bed, but as we
walked by, her nose wrinkled and her eyes
popped open.

"What is that smell?"

"Your nephew Dashiell decided to douse
himself in a new cologne called Eau de
Pisces. He and I are proceeding posthaste
to the bathtub. Would you like to join in
the festivities?"

She crooked her elbow and propped her
head up on her fist. "Um no thanks, but I

think I will get up now and get a cup of
coffee."

Dash allowed me to hoist him into the
tub. He stood with his legs splayed out and
his head hanging low. A more perfect
picture of dejection I had never seen.

I ran tepid water over him and reached
for his bottle of shampoo. Repeatedly, I
squirted the shampoo along his back where
the fish gunk was thickest, and rinsed.
But, time after time, Dash failed my sniff
test. I tried several kinds of human
shampoo and still the foul odor clung to
him.

I always keep a bottle of fancy bubble
bath on hand for life's emergencies, great
and small. The name of this particular
bottle was called Key Lime Sunshine. I
doused him with the stuff, rubbed it in and
again rinsed. Eureka! It worked. Key Lime
Sunshine was a miracle in a bottle.

I lathered the rest of his doggie
parts up, rinsed and then toweled him off
as much as I could. I started to lift him
out of the tub but, squirming out of my
arms, he leaped and bolted out the door.
Dash threw himself on an area rug and
rubbed himself a bit drier. Then he jumped
up, tore through the dining room to the

kitchen, found a rug there and again flung himself on it.

Holding her coffee cup, Marti followed the action with an amused look on her face. While we'd been in the bathroom, she'd lit scented candles all around the house. The air was now heavy with the mixed scents of lavender and jasmine, a big improvement over the aroma of long dead salmon.

Who can say if Dash ran out of dry rugs first or wet fur but he eventually laid down, panting. As for myself, I mopped up the bathroom floor and then changed out of my soaking-wet clothes.

Ten minutes later, Marti and I sat at the kitchen table. She was nibbling on a slice of toast when I looked over at her. "I think I can squeeze in another day off. What do you say to grilling a few more suspects, Crime Solving Partner?"

She studied me. "You think sleuthing is a cure for the lovelorn, don't you?"

I grinned. "I can't think of a better antidote for a snoop such as yourself."

She sighed. Then squaring her shoulders, said, "you're right. I need to buck up. I could sit around twiddling my fingers while I wait for him to come back, but that may not ever happen.

Alternatively, I could use this laser focus that came over me yesterday, for the benefit of mankind. Let's make a plan."

I couldn't help but look at my good friend with renewed admiration. Way to go, Marti Strong-Heart Gonzalez. We decided we'd try the Pembower kids again, but it was only nine o'clock, a little early to call on complete strangers. Marti sat, with a pensive look on her face. I hoped she wasn't sliding back into somber mode.

Instead, she looked up and said, "I've been wondering about that 'Don't Tread on Me' bumper sticker. Do you think it has any deep significance?"

"Hmmmn. I've wondered about that, too. Let's look on the Internet." I walked into my office and flipped on my computer. It turned out that there are all kinds of places that the bumper sticker can be purchased in any color of your choice. Scrolling down past the merchandising sites, I began to see web pages for preppers and other doomsday groups, as well as militias.

Marti was reading over my shoulder. "I wonder if Pembower was with one of these bunches."

"I don't know. There used to be at least a couple of pretty active militia bands around northern Michigan."

Marti nodded. "Yeah, I think I remember hearing about that. Why do you think this beautiful place would be a breeding ground for a fringe element like that?"

"Beats me, but it seems that semi-rural environs like this attract extremists. Maybe it's because people tend to be a little more self-reliant in these areas." I grinned at her as another thought popped into my head. "Then again, maybe it's a side effect of the long, cold winters up here."

I typed in "militia groups, Northern Michigan", hoping that my searching these topics didn't brand me as an anti-administration zealot in a government sweep of Internet data. The only references I found were from fifteen years ago or more. If the militia was still around, it had gone underground. I said as much to Marti. Then added, "Maybe they communicate with each other on the dark net."

She raised her eyebrows. "I suppose that's possible. Do you want to see if they do?"

Hot Dog

"Do you even know how to get on the dark net?"

"No, do you?"

"Should we call our local Internet provider? Tell 'em we want to create some skullduggery? If they can get us hooked up, I'm sure there's an additional charge for it."

"If the Pembower kids prove to be cooperative, we can ask them if the bumper sticker meant that their dad was in some paramilitary group."

I looked at my watch. "By the time we get over to one of their places, it'll be going on ten o'clock. Think that's a decent time?"

Marti shrugged. "I guess. We'll never know until we try." With that, we blew out all of the candles, donned our jackets and made our way to the car.

Chapter Twenty-Seven

We decided to start with Mandy Pembower. On the way over I pondered why we were going to her place first. Was it because her in-town location was closer? Or was it because as a female, she seemed less threatening than meeting up with another male Pembower? Maybe it was a little of each. The main thing was that Marti seemed thoroughly engrossed in our adventure.

Passing a small storefront gave me an idea. "Hey, Marti, she's living in a subsidized rental place and she's a single mom. Why don't we stop at the bakery and pick her up a few muffins?"

"Great idea."

I hung a right turn, went around the block, and into the parking lot of Bagels By the Bay. Opening their front door, cinnamon-tinged air washed over us. We wound up with a half dozen muffins for Mandy and one each for Marti and me along with a mini blueberry muffin for Dash.

We pulled up to the curb outside Mandy's apartment building. I picked up the bag of muffins, and we made our way into the building, up the stairs and to her front door. We rang the bell and a few moments later the door was opened by a young woman in her late twenties.

I smiled, "Hi, my name is Onalee O'Conner and this is my friend Marti Gonzalez. Are you Mandy Pembower?"

She looked back and forth between us. "What do you want?"

"We were speaking with your mom a couple of days ago, and she suggested we talk with you. We knew your dad and we're trying to help the police figure out what happened. I'm so sorry for your loss."

She looked away and fought back tears. She was scrawny and looked vulnerable. I hadn't expected to witness grief with anyone over Pembower's death.

I held out the baked goods to her. "We stopped at Bagels By the Bay and thought we'd share some with you. I hope you like them."

She brushed the tears from her eyes and reached for the bag. "Thank you. My son and I love them," she said and stood awkwardly in the doorway.

Marti broke the uncomfortable silence. "Mandy, we've talked with a lot of people over the past few weeks and we haven't found anyone who seemed to have a real problem with your dad. Have you got any idea who would do such a thing?"

"I'd ask you in to the house but my son's got a bad case of the flu. I wouldn't want you to get it." She looked over her shoulder into the apartment. "He's sleeping right now."

"There's a lot of that going around, I've heard. Does he have the respiratory kind that's been so bad this fall?" Marti asked, flying by the seat of her pants.

"No, it's his stomach. We were up half of the night."

"That's terrible. I hope you don't get it."

Mandy gave Marti a small smile. "Yeah, me too."

"We won't keep you. You look like you're dead on your feet. But, has anything come to you about your dad?" Marti asked.

She looked at the floor. "I don't like to say it but there were times when daddy drank a little too much and he could get a bit testy. I think the neighbors got into it with him a few times." She looked up, "When he was sober he was as sweet as a pussy cat."

Hot Dog

Marti watched her, searchingly. "I know. I have a friend like that, nicest guy in the world until he has one beer too many. I urged him to go to Alcoholics Anonymous but he always said he didn't have a problem and could stop anytime he wanted to." She looked off into the distance for a moment and then back at Mandy. "Unfortunately, one day he had too much, got into an argument with his wife and broke her arm. She wound up divorcing him even though he apologized up a storm and begged her to take him back."

Mandy nodded. "Yup, that's the way it was around home. I learned to stay out of his way when he'd had a few, but Mom never seemed to figure it out. They'd get into it real bad. After my brother, Ger, and I left home, she kind of quit trying to make it work and moved out."

"My friend Eddie is still drinking and I worry about him," Marti added.

"I used to worry about daddy, too." She frowned. "I guess I had good reason to, as it turns out." She looked away as tears welled up in her eyes again. "Have you . . . have you found out anything about . . . about my dad?" She stepped to the side of the doorway. "Come in, I guess it'll be okay."

Marti walked through the door with me on her heels.

The apartment was small but cheerful. "Your place is so cute and homey," I said.

"Thanks. It's all hand-me-downs, garage sale finds and dumpster stuff. My friend Shannon calls me the Dumpster Diva."

"You've done wonders with it," I said, appreciatively. *I read those magazines about budget room makeovers all the time but the home decor on a dime is something I've never mastered. But she has.* We sat on her couch. "You've got a real knack for interior decorating." I looked at her. "Did your dad know you were a dumpster diver?"

"No," she said quickly. "He would've killed me if he'd ever seen me." A look of fear clouded her face. "I mean he'd be really upset. He never, ever, laid a finger on me. He was kind of a stickler for law and order, you know?"

"Sounds just like my dad," Marti said. "He'd embarrass me sometimes when he'd yell at the homeless people in our town."

"Exactly. They weren't hurting him."

"No. What difference did it make if they fished around in the recycling bins for returnable cans? It was no skin off his nose."

Mandy giggled. "I've never heard that expression before. Daddy told me about getting into a fight with a homeless guy a couple of months ago. He was real proud of himself, but I didn't like it."

"You've got a good heart," Marti said.

She shook her head, "I just feel bad for people like that. Daddy was big-hearted, too, it's just that . . . I don't know, he was . . . rigid."

As delicately as I could I asked, "Mandy, one thing I was wondering, would anyone benefit financially from your father's death?"

She looked at me, frowning, "Just my brother and me."

"But, you're living in subsidized housing," I said.

"We haven't gotten the money yet. We can't afford to leave this place on what I make. But, when we do, I plan on buying us a house. Mikey will have his own backyard and a swing set."

"Will you have to keep working?" Marti asked.

"Oh sure. But, I might go back to school, just part time. I'll put the rest of the money in the bank. Daddy would've wanted it that way. He hated lazy people."

"I hope your brother is as sensible as you are."

Mandy looked away. "Yeah, me too."

"Do you think he'll talk to us?" Marti asked.

She pursed her lips together and shook her head. "If he's sober, he'll tell you to get lost. Or worse. If he's drunk, he'll be bat-crap crazy."

Seeing Marti's eyebrows shoot up, Mandy smiled, "Sorry, but he can be really, really nuts."

"Do you see him much?" I asked.

"Not really."

"Were he and your dad close?"

She gave a mirthless laugh. "They couldn't be in the same room together for more than two minutes.

Hmmm. "Is it possible that your brother and dad started arguing and one thing led to another? If they'd both been drinking . . ."

Mandy looked down at the floor. Finally, she said in a small voice, "No, I'm sure that Ger wouldn't hurt daddy."

I glanced over at Marti. She wasn't buying Mandy's assertion either, but we weren't going to get any further with this line of questioning. Time to change the subject.

"Mandy, we saw that 'Don't Tread on Me' bumper sticker on your dad's truck. Was he in a militia group or something?"

She hunched her shoulders together. "Yeah. He didn't like the direction the country was heading in."

Out of the corner of my eye I caught some movement. A small boy stood in the doorway across the room from where we sat. Noticing him, Mandy rose and hurried over. Scooping him up she felt his forehead and studied his face. "How do you feel, sweetie?"

He scowled at us and buried his face in her shoulder.

She looked in our direction. "He's a tired boy. I'm sorry, he's not very friendly today."

"We'll get going," I said, "but thanks so much. Is there anyone else you can think of that we should talk to?"

She wrinkled her nose as she thought. "Maybe his girlfriend?"

Marti caught my eye. How in the world could a scumbag like Pembower have another woman in his life?

"Um, do you know how we could get in touch with her?" Marti asked as we got up and started towards the door.

"Mommy?"

"Sweetheart, I'll just be another minute," Mandy said, jiggling Mikey as she walked with us. "I only met her once. Her name is Mary, something or other. I can remember that because they were Mary and Gerry."

"Do you know where she lives or anything that can help us find her?"

She thought a moment. "I think she works at Johnnie's. I'm pretty sure that's how they met. My dad hung there quite a bit."

I opened the door.

She stepped back, keeping any draft off her son. "Thanks again for the muffins. I hope you catch the guy who did it," she called after us as we walked to the car.

***

As we fastened our seat belts, I turned to Marti. "She sure is different than I expected."

"Yeah, she seems like a nice person and a good mom."

"I know. She must've taken after her mother."

206

Hot Dog

"Good thing."

I turned the key in the ignition. "Want to sample some Up North night life?"

"We're going to Johnnie's, aren't we?" Marti asked grinning.

"Yup. How about tomorrow night?"

"Oh. That's right, you've got a date tonight with Mitch." Her grin faltered and her voice held a tinge of sadness. She was happy for me, but it didn't take much for thoughts of Frank to flood back over her. Maybe I could do something to cheer her up a bit.

Chapter Twenty-Eight

We returned to the O'Conner manse about eleven a.m. I went into my office to do some phoning while Marti cleaned up the kitchen. My first call was to Mitch. I hoped he might be able to rustle up somebody for Marti tonight so we could double date. Of course, a new man wouldn't take the place of Frank, but it would get her out and keep her busy. I didn't feel good about leaving Marti by herself while I was out on the town. Mitch readily agreed and said he'd call back if he found someone.

I made a couple of calls on behalf of my appraisal, checked emails and tidied up my office. By then it was 11:40, close enough to noon that we could justify eating lunch. Marti and I each had a cup of pea soup and a raspberry cheesecake muffin. Dash ate a bowl of kibbles chased by his mini-muffin. It was roughly a 4.9 out of 10 on the healthfulness scale, in case anyone was counting. Just as we were dabbing up pastry crumbs with our fingers, the phone rang. It was Mitch calling back to say he'd thought of someone for Marti. I laid the phone down and asked Marti if she'd come with us.

"On, this smacks of your handiwork."

"Not at all. I guess Mitch was talking with some of his friends around the station, one thing led to another and his buddy wants to go, too. Marti, those policemen lay their lives on the line for us on a daily basis, and if you can provide a bit of cheer for one of them, I would hope you'd step up and do your civic duty."

She glared at me. "All right. I'll go this time but for future reference, I don't need you to arrange my social calendar."

* * *

After the dishes were rinsed and stacked in the dishwasher, we decided to mosey on over to Junior Pembower's house for the second time. Once again, no one was there. "I wish we'd thought to ask Mandy when her brother was usually home."

"Too easy. Private eyes were meant to suffer a bit as they meander along the crime solving trail."

"At the price of gas, these hopeless forays do hurt me."

"It'll all be worth it in the end. You'll see."

***

Around five o'clock, I got Dash's dinner for him. After he'd gobbled it down, I took him for a brief jaunt around the block since we'd be out past his usual walk/bathroom break. Then I washed and pouffed up my hair, selected a cute sweater and turtleneck combo and changed into my best slenderizing, curve-enhancing jeans.

It was about twenty minutes before Mitch and his friend were supposed to land on our doorstep when I poked my head out of the bathroom to check on Marti. She was engrossed in a rerun of a sitcom that hadn't been that great the first time around, and was still wearing the clothes she'd had on all day. I hadn't really noticed it earlier, but training a critical eye on her, I saw lank hair hanging in greasy strings.

"Marti, they'll be here any minute now. You've got to get ready."

She tore her eyes off the TV and glanced over at me, "I'm all set." A laugh track eruption yanked her gaze back to the TV show.

Hot Dog

Apparently funk had once again settled heavily upon her. "Maria Martina Gonzalez". I'd never full-named her before and her head snapped around. "You are not going out like that. Your hair needs washing and there's a big glob of pea soup on your shirt." She pulled her shirt up and found the spot. "Now, you hie on in to the bathroom and make yourself presentable. Maybe this date doesn't mean much to you, but I like Mitch and I don't want him to think my friend is a slob."

"Oh, all right," Marti grumbled.

In remarkable time, she emerged with clean clothes, her hair a shining mass of curls, and the guys weren't due for another two minutes. The doorbell rang, and Dash dashed to the door as I ambled over. Mitch's friend must be ultra-punctual, I thought, remembering that Mitch enjoyed a more casual association with arrival times. As I threw open the door, a hideous possibility washed over me. Why had I not thought this through better? Standing on my stoop, next to Mitch was the object of my dread. Mr. Costas had come a-calling.

As my jaw dropped, the two of them stood there beaming. Dash ran from behind me and romped over to them. Marti slid around me, saw the grinning duo and burst out laughing. I held the door open, and the two men stepped in to choruses of hellos and woofs.

Marti and I donned our jackets and we piled into Mitch's SUV. Casual dining suited us all, and we settled on a bar and restaurant that specialized in pizza with unusual toppings. We ordered one veggie and one meat pie, and four beers. Through dinner, Mitch and Costas regaled us with tales of the most recent misdeeds about town. To hear the two of them talk, it would seem that many of Petoskey's greatest criminal minds are considerably less than rocket scientists.

After our meal, we hoofed it to the library for the movie. At one point Marti and Mitch pulled ahead, engrossed in a conversation about Detroit where the two of them hailed from, and Costas fell in beside me. Uh oh, here comes a snarky comment, I thought.

"Your friend Marti is great. Thanks for letting me join you tonight. This has been fun."

"I'm glad you came," I heard myself say with no insincerity. *Could this be a new chapter in the ongoing O'Conner-Costas saga?*

After the movie and drive home, the two guys walked us to the door. Mitch bent down and brushed my lips with a friendly kiss while Marti and Costas hugged. Later, as we walked Dashiel down the street, I said, "That turned out to be a fun evening. I'm amazed at how entertaining Detective Costas can be."

"Yeah, it was nice, and I do love that movie."

I looked over at her. "You've seen it before?"

"Frank and I went to it a few months ago."

"Geesh, I'm sorry. What a crummy coincidence."

"It's okay. That stuff is bound to happen occasionally."

"You know, Costas said you were 'great'. Maybe we could ask the two of them for dinner next week."

"I don't think so."

"Why not?"

"Because I don't like being a fifth wheel."

"Say what?"

"Didn't you notice that Camille watched every move you made? The guy is smitten with you."

"Is that why he gives me speeding tickets and runs me in for grilling sessions? That's the oddest dating ritual I've ever heard of. No, if you give him a little encouragement, I think he could become very interested in you."

She shook her head and sighed, but I made a firm resolve to engage in some behind the scenes machinations.

Chapter Twenty-Nine

Saturday was a crisp late October day, and Marti and I were in the Honda retracing our route to Junior Pembower's house. Pulling up in front, we saw a pickup truck in the driveway. "Looks like we've struck gold."

"Gold might be pushing it," Marti said, glancing at the unkempt yard.

As we neared the house we could hear a football game, and through the window we saw men in Michigan State uniforms running across a wide flat screen television. Without much enthusiasm, I rang the bell.

A few minutes later, the door swung open and a rather short, swarthy, powerfully-built man glared out at us. I introduced Marti and myself and told him we were looking into his father's death.

"Who are you with?"

"We're not exactly with anyone," I said.

"Then why are you wasting my time?" He began to slam the door but Marti neatly inserted her foot, stopping it from closing. A look of surprise crossed his face.

"Please, could we just ask you a couple of quick questions?" She twinkled at him.

His face darkening with rage, he thrust himself forward stomping on Marti's foot. She screamed. Junior's face twisted into a malevolent grin.

I grabbed for Marti as she fell back against the railing. "Are you okay?"

"Pushy bitch," Junior snarled and heaved the door closed.

Marti's breath was shaky. "Yeah. Let's get out of here." She hobbled down the steps and onto the walkway.

She is one quick limper, I thought, rushing to catch up. Reaching the car, I said, "We should get you home and ice that. Do you think it's broken?"

"I don't think so." She leaned back against the seat and was quiet for a few minutes as I drove back towards Petoskey. "Guess what?"

"What?"

She chuckled. "I've seen my first skirmish as a private eye."

***

Hot Dog

Marti spent the rest of the afternoon with an elevated leg and a good book. The purples and blues adorning her foot looked ugly, but she insisted that it was nothing more than a deep bruise. We were both in the mood for spicy food, so I stirred up a pot of vegetable korma with a side of Sri Lankan potatoes. Soon the luscious scents of curry and cilantro permeated the entire house. It was time to walk outside and stand on my porch for a few minutes, taking in the fresh air and cleansing my nasal palate. It was a blustery cold day, and before long I was shivering. Opening the door, I stepped back inside and became engulfed in the savory smells.

Whenever I looked in on her, Marti seemed content, stretched out in front of a crackling fire in the woodstove. I prepared the vegetables and tipped them into their simmer sauce. About five o'clock, I opened a bottle of cabernet and poured us each a glass. I pulled another chair close to the fire and we toasted her injury in the line of duty.

"What time do you think we should hit Johnnie's?" she asked.

"You still want to go?"

"Does the pope swim? Is a fish Catholic?"

"Is that politically correct, Ms. Gonzalez?"

"I was raised Catholic, so I can say those things. What kind of place is this Johnnie's? Do we need to get there early to avoid a crowd?"

"I haven't been there in years. Let's see if there's anything in the paper about it. I snagged the weekend entertainment section of the paper from my coffee table and perused the listings. "It says, 'Johnnie's, Russ and the Cattle Rustlers Saturday night from nine until one a.m. No cover.'" I looked over at Marti. "They're a local country and western band."

"I figured. Should we get there about eight, before it gets crowded and noisy?"

"Yeah. That's probably the only time we can talk to Mary."

The korma was a new recipe, and though I'd tweaked it with added spices, Marti and I both added generous dollops of coriander chutney as a flavor enhancement. The potatoes, always a crowd pleaser, were as tasty as ever. Over dinner, the biggest topic of conversation was about what to wear to a C and W bar. In the course of the discussion it was revealed that neither Marti nor I had ever owned cowboy boots or western wear. For this evening's attire, we settled on jeans and flannel shirts. *We might not be true C and W women, but we'd at least look C.*

Johnnie's is located on a county road between Petoskey and Harbor Springs. We left my house about 7:45 and pulled into the gravel parking lot just before eight o'clock. There were a half-dozen other vehicles, and nearly all of them were pickup trucks. A light rain was falling and they looked shiny in the light from the lampposts.

Marti and I splashed through puddles on our way to the entrance of The John, as the locals call it. Playing up its nickname, the front door is made of old barn wood and sports a neon half-moon near the top.

Stepping in, the smell of stale beer assailed us. A juke box played an old Lee Ann Rymes song, one of the few country tunes I recognize. A middle aged lady behind the bar glanced up and hustled over to us. Her name tag told us she was Mary. "Hi, folks. You can sit wherever you want but the best seats to see the band are towards the front." She gestured at an area partially set up already with the band's equipment.

"I'm not sure how long we'll be here. We just came in for a quiet drink after a bad day." I said.

"Stay as long as you like." She smiled. "What can I get you ladies?"

Marti spoke up, "I'll have a Molson Ice, please."

"Make that two," I said. A steaming coffee drink sounded really good on this drizzly cold night, but Johnnie's wasn't a fancy drink kind of establishment. While waiting, we looked around the place. What it lacked in charm it made up for in space. There were three couples scattered at the far-flung tables and a few people sitting at the bar.

As we talked, I noticed a man staring at us. I looked closely at him, but he wasn't anyone I knew. Watching, I saw that he followed Mary with his eyes. She brought back two open bottles of beer and set them in front of us.

"Thanks," we both said.

I cast around for a way to converse with Mary and bring up Pembower. I caught her eye. "We were hoping to meet up with an

old friend of ours that we haven't seen for
a couple of months. This is his favorite
place to hang out. Maybe you know him.
Gerry Pembower?"

She looked stricken for a moment then,
with an effort, gathered herself. "Oh,
honey. You must not have heard. Ger is . .
. is . . . dead."

I plastered on a shocked facade, while
Marti made small mewing noises and shook
her head. "He can't be. He looked fine last
time I saw him, and it wasn't that long
ago." Frowning slightly, I looked up at the
ceiling. "It seems like it was around the
Fourth of July and we ran into each other
at the grocery store."

"He got himself killed, sweetie."

"It wasn't a car accident, was it?" I
dropped my voice. "Sometimes he drank a
little more than he should have when he was
driving."

She shook her head and sighed. "No,
somebody killed him. It was in the papers,
didn't you see it?"

Marti and I looked at each other.
"Neither of us take the paper, and we were
both in and out of town in the late summer.
I guess we just missed it." I said. "But, I

do remember hearing something about a murder. That was Gerry, huh?"

"It's such a shame." Marti said. "I hope they caught the guy who did it."

Mary put her hands on her hips. "As a matter of fact, they haven't."

"Did you know Gerry very well?" Marti asked.

She gave her a sad smile. "He was my sweetie. We'd been going out."

"Oh, no! How horrible for you. I'm so sorry," I said.

"Yup. He was something else. He really treated me like a lady, you know?"

Unbelievable, I thought then quickly said, "I do. It's hard to find guys like that. By the way, I'm Onalee, and this is my friend Marti."

"Nice to meet you." She looked down and pointed to her badge. "As you can see, my name's Mary."

"Mary . . . what's your last name? I think Gerry told me about a nice gal named Mary. He thought we'd like each other."

She smiled at me. "It's Ostering. And you are?"

"Onalee O'Conner and Marti Gonzalez."

"Hmmn. I don't remember him mentioning either of you, but we weren't together very long."

"I'm glad we finally met, despite the circumstances." I leaned towards her and lowered my voice. "Why is that guy over at the bar," I tilted my head towards him, "staring at us?"

She glanced over her shoulder. "That's just Jimmie. Pay him no mind. He's a guy I went out with a couple of times. He's a pussy cat."

"Mary, do you have any idea who would want to kill Gerry?" Marti asked.

"The police asked me the same thing. I suppose as the girlfriend, I was probably a suspect. I didn't really have an alibi, since I went straight home after work and was in bed, by myself, when it happened." She shook her head. "But things had been going along so good between us, so why would I hurt my Gerry? I never met his ex, but I heard there was bad blood there." She shrugged her shoulders. "Usually is when there's a divorce, don't you think?"

"Seems that way," I said. "I was kind of wondering about his kids. Did you know them?"

"I met the daughter once, and she seemed like a sweet little thing. I always got the feeling that Ger didn't want me to meet his son. I don't think they got on very well. He didn't really talk about either one of them very much."

"He must have had some feelings for them. He mentioned to me one time that he was going to leave his estate to them."

She raised her eyebrows. "When did he tell you that?"

Oops, sometimes my mouth runneth over. "Um, I don't know. I guess it's been a while, now that I think of it."

"He changed his mind since then. He told me he was gonna get the will changed and leave all his money to the club."

"The club?" Marti asked, puzzled.

"Yeah, you know his militia guys."

"I wasn't aware of that." I said.

"Maybe I'm talking out of school, but that was what he planned on. He was afraid all that do-re-mi would make his kids soft and lazy. He really believed in those Henry-Men of his." She shook her head. "I wasn't too sure about them, myself, but it was his money."

"Had you known Ger very long?" Marti asked.

"Nah. Not really. I just moved up here last spring from Flint. I actually met Jimmy over there at the bar first. Him and I went out a few times, nothing serious. Then I met Ger, and we just clicked. Jimmy and Ger were friends and Jimmy backed off when I started spending time with Ger."

Mary looked towards the bar and noticed the bartender watching her. "Got to go. Johnnie wants us to be friendly but as he says, 'Don't stand around chewing the fat on my nickel.' He's warned me before, and I can't afford to lose this job."

As she hurried away, Marti and I looked at each other. "Pembower was going to change his will? This is an interesting development."

"The big question is whether his kids knew about it," Marti said.

"It sure provides a motive, doesn't it?"

"Man, does it! You know, he may have gotten it changed before he died and it's being contested. That might be why Mandy and Junior don't have the money yet."

Tables around us were filling up, and the noise level escalated. Another waitress had come on duty, and she and Mary had their hands full.

"See anybody you know?" Marti asked.

"Not a one." I noticed Marti had only drunk a couple of sips of her beer. "How long do you want to stay?"

"We've gotten what we came for. I'm ready."

Chapter Thirty

Sunday was stormy and turned into a day of relaxation coupled with cooking experimentation. Lacey and Kitty came over, and while we humans attempted to come up with some delectable soup concoctions for the cook-off, Dash and Kitty romped around the house.

Lacey said she'd met up with Pete and Sydney a couple of times at the beach but had no news to report to us. Marti and I skirted around our recent findings, tacitly agreeing once again to keep Lacey out of the loop.

The two soups we came up with provided a filling dinner but were pronounced by all of us to be unremarkable and certainly not worthy of entrance in the cook off.

After a solemn vow to redouble our efforts, Lacey and Kitty left.

***

For the next several days, I turned back into Diligent Appraiser O'Conner and made significant progress on my appraisal. Marti galloped through two novels and sallied forth on extended bike rides and long walks with Dash. I also saw her staring at a list of suspects we'd put together on one of my yellow legal pads. Apparently, she was trying to find some connection that we'd overlooked. Occasionally she checked her emails but didn't seem to be too distraught over her lack of gainful employment.

I liked having her company, but I thought she might be better off going back downstate to her home and business. Also, I wondered if she hoped that by being in Petoskey she could run into Frank even though she professed that she didn't want to. She might think that one thing would lead to another and he'd drop the floozy and return to her, his true love. I hated to see Marti languishing in a very likely hopeless situation.

Finally, over a dinner of popcorn and cabernet, she broached the subject. "Another great dinner. I'm going to have to start paying room and board if I stay up here much longer."

"Have you bid on any jobs lately?"

"Kind of, but not very aggressively. I guess I got outbid on all of them," she shrugged. "That's okay. They were all crummy and I'm not about to work for pennies on a dollar. What did your old boss used to say?"

"'It's better to go broke fishing than working.'"

"That's right. Life's too short to spend time working for nothing."

"It's just that there's not a ton of stuff to do around here this time of year. I'd hate to see you get bored."

"Thank you for your concern, but I'm just fine." She looked straight at me, eyes sparkling, "I don't think I'll stay much longer, but I do want to be here when we crack the case. It was frustrating being in Detroit when everything came together in our last investigation. This time I plan to be right in the thick of things when it all comes down. I think we're getting closer, I really do."

"Is that why you're sticking around?"

"Of course. Why else?"

"I don't know. I thought it had might have something to do with Frank."

She gave me a scornful look. "You should know me better than to think that I would hang around in the feeble hope of catching a glimpse of Frank the Faithless and his Boomerang Bimbo."

I chuckled. "Great alliteration, Marti. Did that just roll off your lips, or have you been pondering it?"

"I will confess to a teensy bit of fixation with Petoskey's newest Power Couple."

"That's not surprising. At least it's the way I seem to deal with these matters of the heart."

"Oh yes. Don't think I've forgotten the Odious Tim. Any pet names for Rickie Baby?"

"Naw, that just kind of faded away after he moved to the other side of the country. I guess I got dumped, but it was a slo-mo slide. We were involved but not in love."

I was happy to see Marti's interest in the case. I was much better equipped to deal with Marti the overzealous amateur sleuth than Marti the lovelorn. "I've seen you poring over our list of suspects and you say we're closing in on the culprit. Have you come up with something new?"

"As a matter of fact, I was going to mention that you're working too hard on your appraisal. Your lack of detecting time has made you pale and wan, so I have put together a bit of a 'To Do' list. I think we need to tackle it as soon as possible. Can you take a couple of hours off during the next few days? I think it's better if we go as a team."

"First, let me see the list," I said, wanting to keep my options open. She gave me one of her signature combination sigh-glares. I hadn't been on the receiving end of one of those for a long time, and it was good to see her getting back to her old self.

She laid her popcorn bowl on the table, pushed up from the chair, and strode over to where the yellow legal pad was perched on her air bed. As she walked back towards me, she flipped over a couple of pages.

"No. 1. Research both Pembower kids. Find out where they work, what they do for fun, who their friends are, if they owe money and how much."

"Wait a sec. How are we going to find out all of that stuff? You almost lost a foot the last time we 'researched' Junior Pembower. I'm not willing to risk a limb for this, are you?"

"Let me finish the list, please," she said, a bit too officiously in my opinion. Maybe lovelorn wasn't so bad, after all.

"No. 2. Go to the construction company where Pembower worked and talk to some of his co-workers.

"No. 3. Research the ex-Mrs. Pembower, Sharon, and her new husband, Monty Stuart.

"No. 4. Find out more about Pembower's girlfriend, Mary. Why did she leave Flint?

"No. 5. Talk with the homeless guys again, and find out if the one who had the fight with Pembower had an alibi and enough motive to kill him.

"No. 6. Meet some of the militia guys and find out what they're like, what their goals are and how Pembower fit in.

"No. 7. Talk to some of Pete's friends and see if they know anything about the night he snatched Roy.

She looked up from her list. "What do you think?"

"We'd better hire a detective agency."

"Very funny. Which one shall we start with?"

"Let me see the list a sec."

She handed it to me and I studied it. "I say we go where we've gotten the warmest welcome, at least at first. What do you think?" I said, passing the ball right back to her.

"Yup, either that or where we haven't gone before."

"That would be to Pembower's place of work or the militia."

"Exactly."

"We'll try to talk to some militia guys. Let's see what we can find out about them on the web. What did Mary say the name of Pembower's gang was?" I asked.

"The Henry Men."

"That's right." We adjourned to my office and booted up my computer. I typed in, "What is the name of a group of turkeys?"

"Say what?" Marti asked frowning.

"Do you know?"

"No, but—"

"I keep forgetting to look it up, but today I remembered."

"A rafter." I turned my head to look at Marti. "Next time we see one, we'll know."

I clicked out of that screen and typed in *The Henry Men, Northern Michigan*. A website popped up. The homepage featured a circle with the snake, and "Don't Tread On Me quote we'd seen on Pembower's truck. A brief paragraph described the group as "a hometown defense team ready at a moment's notice to help our neighbors when disaster strikes."

As I kept reading, I found out they were named after Patrick Henry, the patriot who, during the revolutionary war, said, "As for me, give me liberty or give me death." Across the top of the website was a menu of choices including photos, videos, "contact us" and links.

"Wow. They're pretty mainstream."

"I know. I thought they'd be more surreptitious."

I clicked on photos. Up came pictures of men with just their first names and hometowns listed. We scrolled through the list. I turned to Marti, standing by my chair. "That's Jimmy from the bar."

She nodded and I moved on down through the names. "I know that guy, too, Scott. He works up at the U-Build store and gave me a lot of great information when I was staining my deck. I wouldn't have taken him for a militia guy. We ought to go talk with him tomorrow." I saw Marti grin.

"Yes! Private Eye O'Conner is back on the case."

Chapter Thirty-One

The following afternoon found us wandering around our local U-Build. I had no idea what hours Scott worked, what department he was typically assigned to or even if he still worked there. So far our searching efforts had been unproductive. We started in the paint department, but not seeing him, we fanned out. I turned to Marti. "He might be on break."

As we entered the plumbing-fixtures aisle I thought I caught a glimpse of him at the other end, but he turned the corner and went out of sight. "Come on, I think that was him," I said and broke into a race-walk, but by the time we got to the end of the row, he was gone. We slowed to our normal pace as we continued our quest. Returning to the paint department, I saw him with a customer over by the display of rollers and brushes.

Scott was a tall man, probably in his forties, with an athletic build. He wouldn't be called handsome by most people, but he had a quiet presence about him that was appealing. As we walked towards him he smiled and said, "Be right with you."

Marti and I looked at the rainbow of paint colors available as he patiently answered the woman's questions. Finally she made her selection and Scott walked with her to where a co-worker was waiting to ring up the sale. Then he returned to us. "How did your deck turn out?" he asked me.

"Great. Thanks for all of your tips."

"You're welcome. Just doing my job. What can I help you ladies with today?"

"Have you got a minute?" I asked.

He looked around him at the mostly empty store. "On Wednesday afternoons in October we aren't usually crawling with people, so what can I do for you?"

Remembering how Marti opened doors for us with her candor, I decided to give truth a chance. "We were interested in the Henry Men and saw your picture on the website. Could we ask you a few questions about the group?"

A slight crease formed between his brows, and he looked away for a moment. When he turned back toward us he asked, "What's the purpose of your questions? Some people hear the word militia and automatically think 'lunatic fringe,' but we're not like that."

I nodded. "I can tell that by the way you do your job here. I think of you as my go-to guy for all things patch-up-able. My friend Marti here and I kind of got involved with the murder of Gerald Pembower." I saw that his frown was deepening, so I tried to explain further. "Some people we know are high on the suspect list, and we're trying to find the real killer to clear their names. We know that Gerald was a Henry Man."

"Yes, he was," he said noncommittally.

"We also saw a picture of a guy named Jimmy, from Petoskey."

Scott nodded again. "Yup, Gerry's buddy."

I looked at Marti for help. Scott seemed willing to answer our questions, but I couldn't think of what I should be asking.

She read my look and flashed Scott a sparkly smile. "We've been told that the Henry Men meant a lot to Gerry. We're trying to piece together what his life was like, hoping we find something that will lead to his killer. Can you tell us what you do when you all get together?"

He studied Marti before speaking. "Mostly we talk about things and drill. The whole point of our organization is to provide an emergency line of defense if there is a crisis. It can be a terrorist attack, a natural disaster or even an environmental catastrophe. We train ourselves so that we'll be ready at a moment's notice if something big like that happens."

"What's the training like?" I asked.

He looked at his watch then at me. "Just a sec." He walked back to the check-out area and spoke briefly with another apronned employee. Then he strode back over to us. "It sounds like this is going to take some time. I can give you fifteen minutes. Come on back to the break room with me."

We followed Scott to the back of the store and through a door, marked "Employees Only". Inside were lockers and a kitchenette. "Want some pop or something?" he asked, using our Michigan name for sodas.

"No, thanks." Marti and I both chorused.

"You're smart to stay away from the stuff. We've also got bottled water in the fridge. Would you like one of those?" He pulled a bottle out. We both shook our heads. "Have a seat." He sat down at the nearest table.

After we were settled, he continued, "Let's see. You were asking about our training. We have drills on disaster protocol. We brush up on our first-aid skills on a regular basis." He looked directly at me then at Marti. "We're required to have a rifle, and there's lots of target practice, but we're not gun-toting fanatics. I had never owned a gun before I joined."

"Why did you join?" I asked.

"It might sound like I'm a worrywart, but we live smack dab in the middle of the fresh water seas. It terrifies me to think of a bunch of wackos deciding to poison our lakes. If that happens and I don't do something to stop it, I'll never forgive myself.

"Plus, we all know that we're close to a long, very open border with Canada, and terrorists can easily slip into the country. If danger ever does strike in these parts, I want to be able to protect my wife and kids."

He came across as a reasonable man even if his was not a path I'd choose. "I can see your point. I'd never thought of it that way," I said, nodding. "Scott, do you have any thoughts on who killed Gerry?"

He frowned slightly again. "Did you know him?"

"A little."

"Then you're probably aware . . . he wasn't the easiest guy to get along with."

"We had a bit of a tiff," I said.

Scott shook his head. "It doesn't surprise me. He was at odds with a lot of people."

"Anyone in particular?"

Scott laughed. "I didn't realize you were this pushy when I was selling you deck stain."

"But you made the sale, and now you owe me," I said, smiling.

He gave an exaggerated sigh, but his eyes were twinkling. "We're not even on commission." He thought a while. "Gerry wasn't my type of person, and I'm sure it was mutual. But we were in the same unit, so our paths did cross . . . Mostly I'd overhear him speaking to his friend Jimmy. He discussed his son some. None of it was good." He paused again and studied the ceiling. "Oh, yeah. He mentioned a woman. I guess he'd started seeing someone." He looked at us again. "You know who you really should talk to is Jimmy. They were best buds."

"How do we find him?" Marti asked.

"I'm pretty sure he still works at Dobbs and Merrick Brothers Construction."

We thanked Scott for his time and let him finish the rest of his break in peace. "Next stop Dobbs and Merrick?"

***

We motored towards the industrial district on Petoskey's south side where Dobbs and Merrick was located. "Jimmy is going to be out on a job site somewhere, so how can we get the receptionist to tell us where he is?"

Marti looked uncharacteristically stumped for a minute. "Good question. Let's see . . ."

After a prolonged silence I glanced over at her. She was staring out the window. "Marti?"

She turned back. "I'm still thinking. With everyone having cell phones, it's hard to come up with a reason for us to not just call him. This is a real poser."

We turned on to Industrial Drive when Marti snapped her fingers. "Okay. How's this? You're Jimmy's sister and you came to town unexpectedly, let's see, from . . . the Upper Peninsula. You only have a little time, because you're traveling on down to Traverse City. Will that work, do you think?"

I tried to think of the pitfalls. "I don't want her to call him because I want it to be a surprise. We aren't real close, so I haven't seen him for quite a while." I looked over at Marti. "In case she wonders why Jimmy never mentioned having a sister."

"Good idea. You're Judith. Judy and Jimmy. I'm your friend who's driving you back home after outpatient surgery."

We pulled into a graveled parking lot outside a pre-engineered steel industrial building. The Dobbs and Merrick Brothers sign was on the front lawn. Marti chuckled as she spotted the topiary of a roaring dinosaur standing guard beside the door.

"I know this building. They dress that fellow up for holidays. He carried an Easter basket on his paw last spring. I'm surprised he isn't sporting his Halloween costume yet."

"I love it. Come on, Judith, let's go," Marti said, reminding me of my assigned role.

A few minutes later we were back in our cars. The receptionist had been reluctant to give us the information, but Marti had improvised. "Is it okay if Judith uses the ladies' room? People need to go to the bathroom frequently when they're on a lot of medications."

"Sure. It's right through that hallway on the right."

"Thanks," I said and hustled to the restroom. I stayed there for a few minutes, noting that the floor was ceramic tile not vinyl and that the sink was in a vanity rather than just hanging on the wall. Dobbs and Merrick were able to spring for decent quality finishes for their offices. In case the receptionist was listening for it, I flushed the toilet and ran water in the sink before rejoining Marti.

"Thanks so much for your help," Marti said, smiling at the lady. Turning to me, "Judith, this sweetheart gave me directions to the job site Jimmy is at today."

"Thank you. You'll never know how much this means to me," I said falling back on my training as a thespian in our fifth grade rendition of "The House on Pooh Corner."

In the car Marti related that as soon as I left the room, she leaned over the receptionist's desk and said in a quiet voice, "Please. We don't know how much time she has left. Those two really need to see each other."

"I told the truth," Marti said. "Nobody knows how much time they have. And, you really do need to see Jimmy."

"Hmmn, it strikes me that you haven't lied yet on these ops."

Marti grinned. "You're right. It's against my principals. If a falsehood is needed, then, you're the woman for the job. That's part of our division of labor."

Team Dobbs and Merrick was the construction crew building a new restaurant south of Petoskey near the highway. "What's our next plan of approach, Truth-Sayer?" I asked as we turned onto the highway.

"That's a good question. Don't you think we can be honest with Jimmy, since we're looking for the killer of his friend?"

"So you'll be doing the talking?"

Marti looked over at me. "Just because you're our designated fibber doesn't mean

you can't chime in with the truth now and
then when the situation warrants it."

"All rightie, then. I'll be on stand-
by alert." We pulled onto the shoulder of
the road near the site. They'd started
construction two months or so ago, I knew
from driving through the area. At this
point, the building was framed in and most
of the work was going on inside.

"Did you appraise this, On?"

"Nope. Wish I had. I like doing
restaurants."

Men went in and out of the building.
We climbed out of the car and wandered over
toward it. As we got to the front door, a
worker emerged.

Marti accosted him, "Excuse me, sir.
We're looking for Jimmy. Do you know where
he's working right now?"

"Yeah, I just saw him. Go through this
door and hang a left." He turned back and
opened the door for us.

"Thanks," we both said and followed
his directions. Inside, the earthy smell of
fresh concrete was all around us. I stopped
and breathed it in.

"Ooh, I love that aroma," I said with
my eyes closed.

"Seriously?"

"Yes. During the past few years, with the recession and no building going on, I really missed it."

"If I didn't know you better, I'd think you were an appraisal nerd," Marti said frowning.

"The nose wants what the nose wants, Marti."

Shaking her head, she started walking again. Soon we spotted our quarry, working by himself.

Marti stepped ahead of me and out came her dazzling smile. "Hi. Are you Jimmy? I'm Marti Gonzalez and this is Onalee O'Conner."

He stopped working and looked at us, eyes roaming up and down our bodies. "I am Jimmy. What can I do for ya?"

Ignoring his roving gaze, Marti plunged on, "We wondered if we could speak to you for a minute. We're looking into the death of Gerald Pembower."

"Oh yeah? I thought the cops had found a guy. One of them animal rights whack-jobs." Jimmy, a brawny man, crossed his arms as he looked at us.

"It doesn't look like he's the right person. Everybody says you and Gerry were great pals," I said.

He nodded. "Yup, him and me were tight."

"I'm sorry you lost your friend," I said.

"Thanks," he said, frowning.

"Have you got any idea who might have wanted him dead?"

Jimmy grinned. "I have to admit, I was amazed when they arrested the animal rights guy. I figured for sure little Junior's paw prints would be all over it."

I raised my eyebrows. "Junior and Gerry didn't get along?"

"Let's just say . . . even I wouldn't want to meet up with Junior in a dark alley. That guy is a nut case. Then, throw in the fact that Ger was changin' his will to cut Junior and Mandy out, and you got yourself a real situation."

"You are a fountain of information," Marti said going into her best butter-up routine and pretending this was new information.

Jimmy gave her a wide grin. "I always aim to please a little lady."

"Anybody besides Junior that you can think of who might have killed Gerry?" I asked before 'the little lady' had a chance to respond negatively.

"There's always that sad sack of an ex-wife of his. Thank the good lord she never got her mitts on any of that money Ger got from the accident," he growled.

"Do you think she'd have any reason to kill him now that she's moved on?" I asked.

"Has she 'moved on'? She had herself a real man before. She's not likely to forget that. Especially since now she's tied down to a wimp." His eyes finally moved up to our faces. "Hey, I seen you two at Johnnie's last Saturday night, didn't I?"

"We were there," said Marti, the high-minded. Still no lies crossed her lips.

"Say, if you gals like country music, The John's having a real fine band coming this weekend. You interested?"

Marti and I looked at each other. "That might be fun," I said, as the designated prevaricator of the partnership.

"I'll pick you up about seven o'clock. We could have dinner at the Tip Of The Mitt Diner first. Make a real night of it."

"Uh, I'm afraid I have to work late that day. But we could meet you at Johnnie's around eight."

"Where do you work?"

"I work for myself. Normally it wouldn't be a problem but I have to be in Gaylord most of the day on Friday."

"Oh? And what is it you do?"

"I'm a real estate appraiser."

"And you have to drive forty miles to do a house?"

"Not exactly. I'm working on an industrial building over there."

"Huh," he said, looking at me, and once again sizing me up. "You must be a real smart girl." He turned to Marti. "What do you for a living?"

"I'm a girl-appraiser, too," she said keeping her tone neutral.

"I'm real impressed. You two sure you want to be seen with a dumb ole redneck like me?"

I curled my lips back into a semblance of a smile. "Oh, I doubt that you're dumb and there are a lot of women who love the challenge of a redneck."

He smiled back, enjoying what he apparently perceived as repartee. "I'd love to keep standing here and chewing the fat with you lovely . . . women, but I have to earn my keep around here. So . . . eight o'clock on Saturday at Johnnie's, right?"

"We'll be there, Jimmy," Marti called out as we left.

"Where should we 'girls' go now?" I asked Marti.

"Yeah, that fried my cork, too. Man, amateur sleuthing sure makes strange bedfellows. Did he give you the creeps?"

"Yup. But, let's not talk bedfellows. Euuuww! Really, would you expect any different from a bosom buddy of Pembower's?"

"No. I'm glad we're not going out to dinner with Jimmy, even if it would give us more of a chance to talk with him."

"We're not getting paid enough for that."

Chapter Thirty-Two

We were a little late for Dash's afternoon walk, so we beelined toward my house. As we pulled into the driveway, we saw him watching for us out the window. By the time we opened the door, he was right there to greet us. He pranced around our legs, catching our eyes.

"Is he grinning at us?"

"Yup. He does that sometimes. He's a happy fellow." Picking up the leash, I yelled, "All good doggies who want to go for a walk, front and center!" He yipped and danced circles around me. I fumbled as I tried to attach a leash to the bouncing dog, but I finally got it. Watching him made me grin, too. *It's all part of the fun of living with a dog.*

As we followed Dash along the street, I asked Marti who her prime suspect was.

"It's not just one. There's a bunch of people still at the top of my list. Let's see, there's Junior Pembower. Anyone who is now or ever was named Pembower is high on the list. There's Sharon, her daughter

Mandy, and Sharon's new husband, Monty.
That's four right there. Then, you've got
possibly, Pembower's girlfriend, the
homeless guy and Pete the dog-rescuer."

Dash stopped at one of his favorite
bushes for an extended sniffathon while
Marti and I waited. Satisfied that he'd
gotten all the news from the bush there was
to get, he lifted his leg and moved on.
Meanwhile, my brain was caught up in the
mystery. "Some of those people don't seem
capable of murder, but I guess you never
know."

"Right. For my money, Junior is the
only Pembower who could kill someone, but
Sharon was abused for all of those years.
Maybe she snapped and got revenge."

I nodded. "The same with Mandy or even
Monty."

We walked to the water's edge before
turning back. The day had turned relatively
warm so I took my jacket off and tied it
around my waist. "Say, Marti, we have lots
of sleuthing to do, but it's a perfect day
to gather kindling for the woodstove. I
think I'll do that after we get Dashworth
here home."

"Need a hand?"

"If you feel like it, sure."

Hot Dog

Thirty minutes later, we drove the Honda with eight large empty boxes in the back, to the wooded area between the street and the bike path. "Be careful of the poison ivy," I said.

"Three leaves, right?"

I pointed with the toe of my shoe. "See that small plant with pretty, cascading white berries?"

"Yup."

"That's it. It doesn't look as much like poison ivy any more, but it'll still pack a wallop if it touches you. There's quite a bit in here, so watch where you step."

We were busy carting out kindling when I saw a man stop in the road by my car. I recognized him as the red- headed homeless man, the one Michael said was named Ron. He watched us for a few minutes. "Gathering firewood?"

"Yes. I have to get a supply of kindling for my woodstove before the snow falls," I picked up the armful I had just compiled. At the car, I opened the back door and placed it in one of the boxes.

"Name's Ron. Want some help? I'm not doin' nothin'."

"Onalee O'Conner. Nice to meet you,"
We shook hands.

"The dog-walker. I've seen you a bunch
of times, though you may not have always
seen me." With that he took off into the
wooded area. Wood snapped as he broke limbs
from dead trees.

I climbed over downed tree trunks and
made my way to where he was quickly
amassing a pile of sticks.

He and Marti had already introduced
themselves. "I've seen you around, too," I
called over to him. "You're a friend of
Tommy's, aren't you?"

He chuckled. "Good old Tommy, man of
few words. Even when he does talk it's
under his breath, sos you can hardly hear
him." He looked over at me. "How do you
know Tommy?"

"I actually don't, but I watched the
police take him away a couple of weeks
ago."

Ron had been pushing hard on the
remains of a spindly tree trunk, trying to
break it off. He stopped and turned toward
me. "You mean you saw when they run him in
for that murder?"

"I think so. It was the day the man
was killed over on Samoset Street." I

stepped on a long branch to break it in two and also test it for dryness. It bent but didn't break so I threw it back. Next year it would be dry enough.

Ron shook his head. "Just because a man's down on his luck don't mean he's capable of murder."

I noticed Marti edging closer to hear better. "You don't think Tommy did it?"

Ron frowned. "I know everybody thinks we're just riffraff because we don't have a roof over our heads, but we're not bad people. We don't do drugs. We don't hurt nobody. We make an honest living picking up after other people." He gathered an arm load of wood and walked past me. "Can you open the car door?"

He hadn't really answered my question. I clambered back over the undergrowth after him. When he'd filled one of the cardboard boxes I shut the car door, and mentioned, "I know that Tommy had a fight a while back with the man who was killed."

Cocking his head, Ron regarded me, "He did? Tommy never told me nothin' about it. Huh. What happened, anyway?"

As we walked back into the woods, I filled him in on the story of Pembower, in the big black truck, yelling at Tommy and shoving him around because he'd caught him removing returnable cans and bottles from the recycling bins.

"What harm is it causing for Tommy or any of us to make a few bucks fishing those cans out of there?" He pursed his lips. "He rode around in his big ole truck with tinted windows. He had a real bad attitude."

I nodded. "But Tommy is scary. I'm not the only one who says that." I examined a piece of birch wood to see if it was too rotted to bother with.

Watching me, Ron said, "That one'll burn just fine. Now Tommy? He sure has a way of looking at you, don't he?" He laughed.

"Yes, and as many times as I've said 'Hi,' to him, he's never done anything except stare at me."

"I know what you mean, but he's harmless. He really is."

"Do you think he had anything to do with Pembower's death?"

"I'd be surprised if he did."

"Do you spend much time with him?" Marti asked.

"Quite often we, ah, camp out together." He gave her a wry smile.

"Were you with him that night?" I asked.

"When was it?"

"It was the night of October Second."

Ron squinted one eye. "I don't know. Let's see." He thought a minute. "My girlfriend was here for a few days right around that time, and I told Tommy to get lost while she was with me." He stomped down on a large limb, breaking it in two. "I'm pretty sure she was still here then. I don't think I can give my boy an alibi. Sorry."

Marti smiled at him. "That's okay. We just need to find out the truth. Where does he spend his nights when he's not with you?"

"I guess you'd have to ask him that," Ron said, grinning back at Marti.

"Will he talk to us?"

"I don't know. Tommy! Get your flea-bitten carcass over here and help us!"

I turned around and, there was Tommy, standing by my car. *How long had he been there, watching and possibly listening to our conversation about him?* He started to pick his way through the tangle towards us, mumbling to himself as he came.

"Tommy, you know these two ladies, at least by sight. This here is Onalee, and that one over there is Marti."

He mumbled some more and then I heard, "the dawg-walker."

I stood where I was, since he didn't seem like the handshaking type. "Hi. Nice to finally meet you."

He gave me one of his hollow-eyed stares, "Yeah. Likewise." Turning to Marti, he said, "Hello."

"Hey, Tommy. You're not doing anything. Help us get some firewood," Ron said.

He glowered at Ron for a minute then started picking up sticks.

"I hear you had a little spat with the black truck guy a few weeks back," Ron said.

Tommy jerked his head around to look at Ron and then, talking to the ground, issued a long string of muffled swear words.

Ron grinned. "So did you do the guy in?"

Tommy picked up the limb he had just broken off from a dead tree, aimed, and threw it at Ron.

Hot Dog

Ron ducked and the wood missed his head by an inch or so. "Guess he don't want to talk about it," he said, chuckling as Tommy stomped off, grumbling to himself.

Marti and I looked at each other. Tommy might be mild mannered, but he was subject to bursts of temper. That piece of wood could have done some real damage to Ron. We worked for a while in companionable silence. Then I said, "Did you ever have any problem with Pembower, the man who was murdered?"

He gave me a lopsided grin. "I did."

"What happened?"

His grin widened. "Which time?"

"Did he hassle you a lot?"

"I guess someone must've appointed him mayor of the area back behind the grocery store. It seemed like as long as I stayed on the bike path and kept on walking, he didn't do nothin'. But on rainy days sometimes, me and Tommy liked to hang out in that gazebo and maybe drink a beer or two. If he saw us in there, he'd come over and yell and push us around."

I watched him as he spoke. "What did you do?"

"I'm not a fighter. Either is Tommy." He laughed. "Though, I guess if he has a stick handy, why, he'll throw it. When the black truck guy showed up, we'd just leave. Of course that meant we'd get soaking wet in the rain." He shook his head. "I could understand I guess, if there were families wanting to use the gazebo for picnics. But on cold, rainy days? Come on, there's nobody. Besides, we've got as much right to use it as anybody." He watched me for a moment. "Here, let me try to break that for you."

He climbed over a stump and picked his way over to me. Grabbing on to the thick branch, he pressed down hard on it with his foot. It broke in two and he handed me both pieces.

"Thanks."

"Gee, Ron, now it sounds like you had a motive to kill Mr. Pembower, too." Marti said.

"I probably did." He grunted as another big limb broke under his foot. Picking it up, he looked over at her. "I would guess that I'd have to stand in line for the honor." He laughed. "Maybe even behind Tommy boy."

We gathered more wood as Ron kept up a steady stream of conversation. Eventually, I took an arm load of wood to the car and dropped it into a container. Marti, following me out of the woods, filled the box. "That does it," I said.

Ron brought another five or six pieces out, and I managed to find room for them. "Thank you so much for your help." I reached into my wallet to pay him.

He put his hand up palm out, to stop me. "You don't owe me nothin'. It was nice to have something to do for a change."

We bantered back and forth, and he eventually took the money. Marti and I hopped in the car and drove home. "We managed to kill two snakes with one stone, eh?" Marti and I had each had parakeets when we were kids and decided to modify the old axiom about birds and stones to our taste.

"Yes, we did. The best part was actually getting to talk with Tommy after all this time. I wonder if he'll speak to us from now on or if he'll revert to his former ways."

"Yeah. It's kind of funny, the way he talks under his breath all the time, but he doesn't seem as scary now."

Pulling in the drive, I saw a man sitting on the porch steps. When he looked up, I realized it was Frank. I glanced over at Marti, who was staring out her window at him. I parked the car and Marti croaked, "Come on. I'll help you get that wood in the garage."

"It can wait."

Frank stood up but didn't come over. He was staring intently at Marti. Meanwhile, Marti, ignoring him, hurried to the rear of the car and struggled with the latch of the hatch back. I walked back, aimed the key fob at the door and it popped open.

Frank loped over to us. "Marti, can we go somewhere and talk?"

She turned towards him and said in a frosty voice, "Anything you have to say to me can be said right here."

I backed away to give them space.

"Stay right where you are, Onalee." Marti commanded, hands fisted on her hips and dark eyes snapping.

I hovered behind her. As a longtime student of body language, I'd say Frank's chances didn't look too good. "Hi Frank."

Giving me a sheepish smile, he returned the greeting. He turned to Marti, and eyes pleading with her, said, "I was wrong. I've missed you so much. Would you please give me another chance?"

Hot Dog

"So that six months or two years from now, even ten years, you can toss me aside when another hot tamale comes to town that you want to make time with? You really think you can just waltz right in here and everything will go back to the way it was? No. I'm telling you right now, no. Fidelity, Frank. That's the word of the day." She turned abruptly and plowed right into me.

My legs shot into the air and I landed on my keister. Frank's and Marti's lips formed wide O's of surprise. Marti reached her hand down to pull me up, mumbled an apology, and rushed past Frank, up the porch steps, and into the house using a spare key.

"Are you okay?"

"I'm fine," I said, brushing off my jeans. I looked into Frank's troubled eyes. "How are you?"

He looked away. "I've been better."

"Don't give up on her, Frank. She's worth whatever it takes to win her back."

He looked at me searchingly. "Do you really think I have a chance?"

"I hope so. But if you ever two-time her again, know this. I will tackle you and

Connie Doherty

stuff both feet down your throat, toes
first."

Chapter Thirty-Three

After Frank slunk away, I opened the front door. Dash, waiting at the threshold, barked an excited, "Hello." I heard noises emanating from the bathroom. Was Marti crying? I knocked on the door. "Hey, are you all right?"

"I . . . I'm fine," she said and I heard the unmistakable sound of heavy guffawing.

Throwing open the door, I saw Marti sitting on the floor, shaking with laughter. Tears streamed down her cheeks. She looked up at me. "The one time I get to make like a drama queen and you go stealing the scene by toppling over on your back, legs . . . legs . . . poking straight up." She shook her head, and there were more peals of laughter. "I had to get out of there."

"First of all I didn't then, nor do I ever, topple. You slammed into me. And now you have the nerve to laugh about it? Secondly, you ripped into poor Frank just so you could create a scene? Shame on you, Marti G."

She wiped her eyes. "I have every right to make that lad squirm. He broke my heart. And as for your incident, you know good and well I inherited the unfortunate trait of finding falls funny. If my mom or my grandma were here, they would still be rolling on the floor." She thought a moment. "What really got me were those feet sticking straight up towards heaven. Come to think of it, your toes were even pointed like a ballerina."

***

The following morning, Dash and I hit the trail by ourselves while Marti answered emails. Then I moseyed over to Gaylord and spent a few hours inspecting industrial buildings. Later in the afternoon, the doorbell rang. Marti, Dash, and I all bounded over to answer it and there stood Frank with an armload of asters and mums. It was a riot of fall color.

Over Dash's barking, Frank asked, "Miss Gonzalez, will you do me the honor of going to dinner with me tonight to the Indian River Inn?"

There was a pause such as what is often referred to as pregnant. All eyes were on Marti. Even Dash swung his head around to stare at her. I didn't dare move for fear of stealing another momentous scene from her.

Finally, she sighed and said, "All right."

I let my breath out then winked at Frank. "Wow, Marti, the IRI is one of our poshest restaurants. You'll be in high clover tonight."

Frank handed the bouquet to Marti. "Thanks. What time should I be ready?" she asked.

I left them to finalize their plans, but Frank didn't linger. I imagined they were still awkward around each other. A few minutes later, Marti stepped back into the house, admiring the blooms.

"Marti. Did you bring any gorgeous gowns up with you?"

"A better question would have been, 'Do you own any dresses?' Then I would have answered no."

I looked at my watch. "We've got time to scour the town. Let's go."

She hit her forehead with the palm of her hand. "Wait a sec. We're supposed to meet Jimmy tonight at Johnnie's. I can't go with Frank." She found her cell phone and was punching numbers in.

I reached out and grabbed her wrist. "Stop. You need to be with Frank tonight. I'll go by myself to meet up with the Jim at the John. He might open up more one on one."

"I don't know. He's creepy."

"Don't worry. We'll be in a big crowd of people. Besides, I wasn't planning on staying out late."

She protested again, but I talked her into it. We bustled out the door.

Three resale and two clothing stores later, Marti had a sapphire blue dress that turned my pretty friend into a knockout while still coming off as understated elegance. I suggested she go for slinky but she said, "Nope. This is basically a first date, and I want my clothes to say that I'm an accomplished woman of the world, not a sex kitten."

"You've definitely got that in spades. You'll have Frank wallowing at your feet."

She smiled. "Thanks, but you're my best friend. You would say that."

"Maybe, but I'll swear on my HP financial calculator that I'm telling the truth."

Hot Dog

***

In a navy blue suit, Frank arrived at six-thirty. I went to the door, feeling happy at this turn of events. When Frank saw Marti standing just inside the door, his mouth opened. "Whoa. You look wonderful."

She flashed him a smile. "Thanks." She'd borrowed one of my dressy wraps, and as she began putting it on, Frank rushed to her side to help her with it. They left with a chorus of good byes. I sure hoped things worked out for them.

I took Dash for a quick jaunt around the block and then dressed for my evening out. I slipped into my sky blue corduroy shirt and jeans. I wanted my apparel to say, "No nonsense. Approachable but not kissable."

Thinking that Jimmy would be fearful of a no-show and very agitated if I arrived at my usual twenty minutes late, I made a super human effort to arrive five minutes early. Actually, I strove for twenty-five minutes early. That way I made it to the John within my personal twenty minute window.

As soon as I walked through the front door I was greeted by Mary, who waved and called out, "Hi, hon." With a bar cloth in her hand, she pointed to a table in the far corner. "He's been waiting on you."

Uh oh. They must've talked, and I hadn't been entirely truthful with Mary. I made my way to the table.

He smiled. "You came. But where's that other pretty little thing?"

"She couldn't make it."

"Well, then, pull up a chair. Just you and me can still have a good time, though I was looking forward to every man in this joint seeing me sitting with two lovely ladies." Grinning at me, he took a swig of beer.

Mary hurried over.

"What's your pleasure?" Jimmy asked me.

I glanced over at Jimmy's bottle. Guessing that he was an adamant buy-American kind of guy, I said, "I'll have a Bud, too, please."

"You can't beat Yankee beer, eh?"

Mary hurried off to get my drink. Hopefully, she hadn't remembered that we'd ordered Canadian Molsons last week.

Jimmy leaned forward, "So you and your buddy were old friends of Ger, Mary says."

I felt my cheeks redden. They had talked, but maybe the truth would work here. "Yeah, as we mentioned to you the other day, we've been looking into Gerry's murder. We didn't exactly tell Mary the truth."

"That wasn't very nice, now, was it?"

I met his eyes. "No. The end never justifies the means."

"I don't know if I'd go so far as to say that, but in this case it don't. Mary is a nice gal, and she's real sad about losing Gerry."

"It sure seems that way. Now, you mentioned that you thought Junior might have done it?"

He narrowed his eyes. "That boy's trouble. I told you that Ger was going to change his will. He wasn't going to leave them one thin dime, and that wouldn't have helped ole Junior pay off his gambling debts."

"Gambling debts?"

"Oh yeah. Big time. The slot machines have a real hold on that boy. I seen in the paper that his house was in for foreclosure and I heard he's run his credit cards up into the thousands in debt. How stupid can you get?" He looked to me for confirmation.

I shook my head. I'd known people with gambling addictions, and it was heartbreaking. "It's very sad."

"Lack of character is what it is. I don't feel sorry for him. He's a two bit pissant. Unless they can hang this thing on him, why, I think he's going to get half of his daddy's loot."

Mary dropped off my beer and hurried off to another table. It was ice cold and the first sip tasted good.

"What about Mandy? She'd have the same motive as her brother, and it looks like she could use the money, too."

He nodded. "Yeah, she's got that kid, and a crummy job, but I don't think she'd have the gumption to kill anybody. Ever met her?"

"Yes, I did. She seems like a sweet person."

"Yeah. Dumb as a box of rocks, according to her dad, but nice." His eyes narrowed again. "Why are you so interested in this? That's what I want to know."

Sticking with that elusive commodity, the truth, I said, "We have a good friend who got mixed up in all of it, and we're trying to help her out."

"By poking your nose into a murder investigation? Makes no sense to me. You go around cross-examining people, you could wind up in a world of hurt."

"This girl's mom was a good friend of mine who died several years ago, and now the kid's got nobody." It seemed best to leave out the fact that Marti was an adventure-seeking p.i. wannabe. I took another sip of my beer and Jimmy took a large swig from his bottle.

"You're one of them do-gooders, I guess," he said, shaking his head.

"That's probably a stretch, although I was a girl scout, briefly. You think Junior is a strong suspect. What about Mary, his girlfriend?"

"Don't seem likely unless they got into some lovers' spat."

Mary was talking with people at the table next to ours, so I moved in closer and lowered my voice. "Mary told us that she used to go out with you."

Jimmy moved his beer bottle aside, leaned in and smiled. "Yup. She did, and we had a lot of fun, but then she met Ger. I could see right away that they was hot for each other. Me and her was more or less buddies, you might say. I told the two of them to go for it, with my blessing."

"That would really bother me."

He frowned. "What, to see your best friend happy? The way those two was going at it, I figured I'd be best man at a wedding before the year was out." He drained the last of his bottle.

We were both still inclined over the table and talking in low tones. I dropped my voice even lower. "You'd said that Gerry was going to leave his money to the Henry Men. Is that true?"

Jimmy's frown deepened. "That's what he told me, but I don't know if he'd gotten around to doing anything about it." He shook his head. "I hate to see half of his dough wind up in the slot machines, especially when it could do so much good."

"You mean by going to the Henrys?"

"Exactly." He moved even closer and fixed his gaze on me as I leaned back a bit. "There may come a time, in the not too distant future, when the Henry Men are all that stand between a band of terrorists and our friends and neighbors. Do you realize how open that border is that we have with Canada, just ninety miles from here?"

Hot Dog

"Is that the purpose of the Henry Men?"

"Sure is. We keep ourselves trained so that we can protect our backyard in the case of an emergency." He regarded me for a moment then said, "I hope I'm not wasting my time talking to one of them anti-gun fanatics."

"No, no. I like to target shoot with pistols. I'm not a hunter, though."

"Say the word, and you and me will go out shooting some time." He grinned, "I think a woman with a gun is sexy."

I sure hoped Marti was having a good time, because I could've really used her and her snappy rejoinders about now. As it was, I was at a loss for words. Ignoring that comment, I moved on, "You also mentioned Sharon, Gerry's ex, as a suspect. Do you know her very well?"

He sat back and crossed his arms. "Alls I know is that she was always riding Gerry. If it was up to her, he wouldn't have had any fun at all. She expected him to work his fingers to the bone to provide for her and the kids and then give up all of his leisure hours doing for her and the family. That just wasn't Ger's style. He was a big picture kind of guy." He motioned to Mary and she came over to the table. "I'll have one more here and get another for my lady friend."

"Um, thanks, but none for me just yet. I'm a slow drinker and I've got quite a bit left." I raised my bottle to show them how much beer I still had.

After Mary left, I resumed, "Gerry and Sharon had been divorced for a while. Do you think she'd have had any reason to kill him?"

He shrugged. "Who knows?" He moved in closer again. "You want to know what I think? It's always stuck in her craw that Gerry came into all that money after they was divorced and she got none of it. That was a hell of an accident," he said shaking his head. "It really messed Ger up, and he could never work again. He deserved every dime he got off that old man."

"That's a shame," I said and meant it. Even a lowlife like Pembower didn't deserve all that pain and suffering. "Sharon wasn't in his will, was she? She wouldn't have any motive to murder him."

"Negatory. Ger never actually said Sharon was written out of the will, but judging by some of the things he did say, I've got to believe she was. He had his new

girlfriend and life on easy street, and
that probably just killed Sharon. I could
definitely see her getting in a hissy fit
and maybe even being mad enough to do him
in."

"Was Gerry abusive to Sharon?"

"Well-l-l-l. I wouldn't say he was
what you call 'abusive'. He may have
slapped her around a bit, but I'm here to
tell you, that woman would have driven St.
Peter to drink."

The John was filling up around us.
Band members walked back and forth carrying
equipment as Jimmy reminisced about old
times with Gerry. The two of them had gone
to the same school and played football
together in the small town of Wolverine,
east of here. After high school, they'd
decided to come to the big city of Petoskey
to seek their fortunes. I was here to learn
about Gerald Pembower, and that I did.

He and Jimmy had been drinking buddies
since they were about fourteen, when they
had split their first bottle of Boone's
Farm wine. Gerald had a weakness for
Snickers candy bars and brats. Of course,
all this talk about Gerald was interspersed
between Jimmy's exploits. Jimmy was a Glock
man but Gerry loved his snub nose. They'd

both been in a militia years ago, until it had disbanded. When the Henry Men started, they'd jumped at the chance to join. "I really miss the guy. He was like a brother to me," he said almost shouting now to be heard over the band.

The music sounded like rockabilly to me, and the dance floor was filling up. "Will you do me the honors?" Jimmy asked.

Oh no! "What?"

"Will you dance with me?" he yelled.

I frowned slightly "I still can't hear you," I yelled.

Jimmy got up, grabbed my hands and pulled me to my feet. Soon we were dancing to the music. I'd almost forgotten how much fun it was. Jimmy grinned at me and I smiled back. We stayed on the floor for three more songs then a slow dance came. *Uh oh, I should've gotten off the floor while the getting was good.* Jimmy reached over and pulled me close to him. We moved as one to the sad refrain about a long lost love and the hills of Tennessee. I closed my eyes and thought of the Odious Tim and Rick, my last two better-off-withouts.

Marti and Frank crossed my mind. I hoped that at least they could make it. Finally my mind drifted to Mitch. I opened

my eyes and looked up. Holy catfish! Mitch
was right beside us, staring at me with a
sheepish grin on his face. His arms were
wrapped tightly around a woman whose back
was towards me. He gave me a half wave and
then twirled away from us. My list of B-O-
Ws just increased by one.

Chapter Thirty-Four

We danced to a couple more songs before
sitting. Jimmy gulped down his beer and
raised his arm signaling Mary to bring him
a refill.

I put a five-dollar-bill on the table
for my beer and tip. "Jimmy, it's been a
long day and I think I'm ready to go. Thank
you for a fun evening!" I had to shout over
the band as I stood and put my jacket on.

He got to his feet.

"You don't have to leave."

He grinned. "I wasn't plannin' to, but
I will walk you to your car."

"No need to, I'll be fine. Thanks
again," I said and turned to go.

Back at my place, Dash greeted me with
his usual zeal.

I whisked him out for a quick walk
around the block. Marti wasn't home yet,
and I took that as a very good sign. I
opened a paperback that had been partway
down on my TBR pile and read for a couple
of hours. Still no Ms. Gonzalez, so I
turned off my light.

Hot Dog

The following morning, I tiptoed past Marti's inert body on the air bed and turned on the coffee maker. After two brimming mugs of coffee, I dressed and pulled Dash out the door. Throughout this time, with a beeping coffee maker, rustling clothes, zipping zippers, and scritching dog nails, Ms. Gonzalez slumbered on. Sigh. I would have to wait to get my update on the state of the reunion.

The D-Dog and I had a pleasant but uneventful stroll, running into no other dogs or humans. Arriving back home, we saw that Marti was up at last, and from the sounds of running water, it appeared that she was taking a shower. I made my way to the kitchen and started a second pot of coffee. Pulling a plastic storage container of sour cream cherry muffins out of the freezer, I set them on the counter to thaw a bit.

Marti was still in the bathroom, so I turned on my computer and answered some emails that had accumulated in my inbox. I heard the bathroom door open.

"There's hot coffee in the kitchen and muffins on the counter, but heat them in the microwave for a bit," I called over to her.

"Thanks, On. Sounds great."

I finished a response to a friend in Colorado, checked the weather forecast and turned off the machine. Marti had to have had at least a partial mug of caffeine by now and would be ready for grilling. I walked nonchalantly out to the kitchen and poured myself a half cup of coffee. Marti was already sitting at the table.

"Golly, I didn't even hear you come in last night," I said getting the conversation rolling. I was in the process of sitting down when she leapt to her feet and thrust her hand at my face. I caught a glimpse of a glimmer on her finger as I fell back into the chair. My jaw dropped as my eyes rose to meet hers.

"Yes! Yes! Yes!" She said, nodding and grinning.

"But—"

She sat down again. "I know, it's sudden. But then again, it's really not. I'd thought we were headed this way until his old girlfriend came back."

"What happened with them?"

"They tried to make it work but Frank says that he'd moved on. He was in love with me and didn't want to stay with her, even though she was willing to live up here with him. She doesn't like it here, not enough shopping I guess. Anyway, his heart wasn't in it anymore, and he told her it was too late. Their time had come and gone.

"Last night he said, 'I know this is quick but I can't wait any longer. Will you marry me?' He was down on one knee and holding the ring out to me."

"In the restaurant?"

"No, we took a walk down by the river after dinner." A thoughtful look came into her eyes. "Maybe I should've played harder to get, but the truth is, I really do love him. I want to spend the rest of my life with him."

"Then, I'd say that you did the right thing." I got up and hugged her. "Have you set a date yet? Wait! Does this mean you're going to move up here?"

"We're leaning towards early next summer. Is there room for two commercial real estate appraisers in Petoskey?"

"Not really." Seeing her frown I added, "Now's the time to live your dream and open up a private investigator firm."

"Ooh, and we could be partners. O'Conner-Gonzalez and Associates. How does that sound?"

"My name's first, now?"

She grinned. "Of course. You've got better name recognition, for now, in this part of the state."

"That sounds like fun. Actually, you'll do fine hanging your appraisal shingle up here."

"Ha, I knew it. You just wanted to keep all the business to yourself. That is so like a bridesmaid."

It was my time to grin. "Say what? Am I going to be in your wedding?"

"Of course, though it may just be a few people on Frank's porch."

"That would be fine. You don't want a big wedding?"

"Nope, never did, but Frank and I haven't really talked about it yet. He or his family may." She paused, then said, "That's my big news. Now, how was your hot date last night?"

I filled her in on everything Jimmy and I had discussed.

Listening intently, she said, "We need to step up the pace of our investigations. Who do you think we should concentrate on?"

"Let's start with the guy we all love to hate, Junior Pembower. Is your foot healed up yet?"

Hot Dog

"Very funny. I'll keep my distance from him this time."

We started by doing some research on the computer. Searching through past editions of the newspaper, we found foreclosure notices for his house, just as Jimmy had said.

"Do you know anyone who frequents the casino and can tell us if Junior is usually there?"

I thought for a moment. There were three or four people I knew who gambled. "Unfortunately, I don't think any of the gamblers I know would be acquainted with Junior. I wouldn't think that anyone who works at the casino would be able to tell us. They must have some kind of privacy policies."

"Yeah, seems like it. Let's go up there and see if he's there."

"Now?" I said and Marti nodded. "It's Sunday morning. Nobody would get up on a Sunday morning and go to a casino."

"I'd guess that he lays around and watches football all weekend, but there are no games on Sunday morning, at least in this time zone. So what does a compulsive gambler do with a free morning?"

"Hmmm, you've got a point, Detective Gonzalez."

We drank the last of our coffee and motored to the Northern Stars Casino. It was a radiant morning, and Little Traverse Bay sparkled beneath a forget-me-not blue sky. We passed a few runners and dog-walkers, but the town was under the quiet of a Sunday morning. Driving past the outskirts of the city, we turned into the parking lot of the casino.

"Wow, On, look at all the cars."

"That's why the town is so empty. Everyone is here."

Opening the door, we walked into the gaming area. We heard soft electronic music and the rhythmic clacking of people playing the slot machines. Nearly everyone smoked as they sat in front of their machines. "Want to try your hand?" I asked Marti.

"No. I'm too tight-fisted with my money. Do you?"

"Me neither. I guess we should stroll around and see if we run into somebody we know."

We meandered along the row of machines and players until Marti stopped abruptly and grabbed my arm. I followed her line of sight and there was good ole Junior Pembower.

"What do we do now?" Marti hissed.

"I think we should keep walking. It's too bad there isn't a machine open beside him."

"Yeah. Then maybe I could get my fingers crushed, too."

"Solving crimes isn't all giggles and grins, Missy."

"So I've noticed," Marti said icily. We were past Junior now and I saw a woman from my neighborhood.

"Hi, Janet. How are you?"

She swung around. "Oh, hi, Onalee. I've been better. This machine is not treating me right." She deposited another token. "Arghghghgh. It isn't my day." She got out of her chair. "I need to rake some leaves today anyway." She turned towards the door. "Nice seeing you, Onalee."

"Wait, Janet." I caught up to her with Marti at my heels. "Do you see that man over there in the Detroit Lions tee shirt?"

"Yes." She'd stopped and was studying me. "What about him?"

"Do you know him?"

"Not really, but I see him up here a lot. Stay away from him, Onalee. I'm afraid he's not a nice person."

"Why do you say that?"

"You're not a friend of his, are you?"

"No, not at all, but I'd like to hear your impression of him."

"More than once, I've watched him give the waitresses a very hard time. I think that says a lot about a person."

I nodded. "Is there anything else you've noticed about him?"

"Just that he's always by himself. Although, I guess that's not unusual in a place like this."

"Thanks, Janet. That's good to know. I'll tell my friend Sue not to even think about dating him." We all walked out, and Marti and I got in my car.

"I guess we don't know any more than we did before, but at least we've gotten our impression of Junior confirmed," I said as we drove down the hill and into downtown Petoskey.

"Yup, and we know he gambles, just like Jimmy told us," Marti said. "What's next?"

I thought for a moment. "One of the items on that list of yours was that we should go talk with some of Pete's pals. Lacey told me once that he lives with his friend Zack at the end of Logan's Lane. Let's go there now. If we're lucky Pete won't be home, and we can talk to Zack in private."

I turned the corner and we headed back towards the south end of town. We spotted Logan's Lane running off River Road and turned down it. It was gravel, and the sprinkling of houses on it were situated beneath large trees. At the end was an old house with grey asbestos shingles. Someone had enlivened the facade with bright blue trim, and it looked cute. We noticed wood smoke curling from a metal chimney on the side of the roof.

We climbed out of the car and made our way down a stepping stone walkway to the front door. After a couple of raps and a lot of barking, the door opened. We looked up at a tall man with red hair and freckles who gave us a questioning look.

"Hi. Are you Zack?"

"Yup. Do I know you?"

"No. My name is Onalee O'Conner, and this is my friend, Marti Gonzalez."

He was smiling. "Lacey's friend! You helped us with Roy. Come on in." He turned and started back into his house. "Pete's not here right now."

"That's okay." We followed him into the house. The living room furniture consisted of a large screen TV, a couch with a slip cover on it and two recliners. We heard more barking.

Zack sat in one of the recliners. "Sorry. That's our latest rescue. He's not well socialized yet, or I'd bring him out to meet you."

Marti and I took the couch.

"What can I do for you?"

"Well," This was kind of delicate. "As you may know, we're looking into the Pembower murder. We wondered if you could tell us what you know about that night."

Zack nodded his head. "I see." He thought a moment. "What is it you want me to tell you?"

Marti chimed in, "We know that Pete and Lacey went over there that night to get Roy and that they got into a fight with Pembower."

"Yup. That's what they told me."

"Lacey says that after that, they went to her house. Then Pete went back there by himself and took Roy away." I watched Zack carefully as I spoke. He was looking away from us. "Do you know what happened when he went back there?"

"Why are you playing detective?"

"Lacey's mom was a friend of mine, Lacey is our friend and she really has no one to look out for her."

"Are you wondering how involved Pete really was with the killing?"

Marti and I looked at each other. "I guess that is what we're fishing for, but I hate to say it. We really like Pete."

"Look, I know from what Pete and Lacey have said that you're good people. Honestly, Pete and I are like brothers. But, I don't know." He shook his head. "He seems different. Something happened that night, but he's not talking about it. At least not to me." He paused then turned anguished eyes on us. "He couldn't have killed him, could he?"

"It doesn't fit with the gentle guy I know either." I said.

We talked a few more minutes then left. In the car I said, "I don't think we can cross Pete's name off our list of suspects."

"I know. What if he is the murderer, On?"

"Lacey will be broken-hearted."

"And she may be involved."

I sighed. "Perhaps being detectives isn't our strong point."

"I guess we should both stick to appraising. We suck as private eyes."

"Stick to appraising, Ms Gonzalez? Have you even written a report this quarter?" I asked with appropriately arched eyebrows.

"Yes, I have, but it has been a while since I hopped aboard the old PC and punched out an appraisal." She paused then added, "I still remember the basics, On."

I looked over at her and smiled appreciatively. "Marti, I'm glad that you're up here now and will soon be here permanently."

"Thanks. Me too. Now, about this case—

"I don't know. We've eliminated a few suspects, but we really haven't made much headway. Maybe we should give it a rest for a couple of days."

At home I had a message from Ginger asking me to observe tradition and come to her house tomorrow evening for Halloween. With only a few little kids in my neighborhood, I've always gone to Ginger's to give out candy on one of my favorite holidays. Calling her back, I said I'd love to come, and I'd bring dinner.

After hanging up, I said, "Marti, I need to go to the farm market and buy some ingredients for dinner tomorrow. Want to come?"

"Sure."

We drove up and down hills through the last vestiges of the orange, red and yellow trees. Turning to go down the drive to Ray's Market, we looked out over the heaping mounds of squashes and pumpkins, down into the valley, across a blue pond and up the faraway hill on the other side.

"It looks like the Scottish countryside. It's beautiful, On."

I selected a plump pie pumpkin, a bunch of radishes, a half-bushel of Honeycrisp apples and the bargain of a lifetime, a bushel of cabbage for $7.95.

Later, at home I began preparations for my batch of pumpkin soup. Marti left with Frank for a walk along the beach and a late lunch. I happily settled down to a long afternoon of cooking. I planned to serve my soup tomorrow, in the pumpkin in honor of Halloween with a side of slaw and an apple crisp for desert.

Chapter Thirty-Five

Holding a pumpkin full of hot soup, I
knocked on Ginger's door. She threw it
open. "I'm starved! I've been hungry for
hours, and I don't dare start eating the
trick-or-treat candy or there won't be any
to give out. Happy Halloween!" She gave me
a big hug.

With Ginger's help, I got the rest of
the dinner from my car and we sat down to
eat. We couldn't tarry too long over our
suppers, because the kids would start to
come at six o'clock, the official start of
trick-or-treating.

It was a chilly night and rain fell
steadily at times, and at other times in
torrents. Ginger and I both predicted that
our number of trick-or-treaters might be
down this year because of the foul weather.

A little before six the doorbell rang,
and we saw two minions and a pirate on the
doorstep. After grabbing their treats and
thanking us, they all skipped down the
steps, and another group of children surged
up the porch stairs. For the next hour we

served up candy to a little girl dressed as a birthday cake, a pint-sized white bunny, more minions, an angel, a headless person and many other assorted creatures.

When we had a break, we decided to take turns walking over to Mitchell Street to see the real action. Five blocks are closed off to traffic and the area swarms with kids and their parents on this festive night. Ginger was first to venture forth and came back with tales of elaborately decorated homes and throngs of people.

I grabbed my umbrella and splashed down the dark street. As I rounded the corner onto Willow Avenue I saw lots of people ahead on Mitchell, but the street I was on was quiet. Rain danced on the pavement and glistened under the streetlights. Low clouds scudding before the wind blotted out the stars and quarter-moon. I turned onto Mitchell and wove through the happy families.

Kids waited in line to walk up to a porch festooned with demons swinging from the eaves. At another house, the strains of eerie organ music emanated and a ghostly purple and black horse-drawn carriage decorated the front lawn. These homeowners spent a lot of time and money welcoming the little kids of their community on this magical night.

At Woodridge Street I turned around and began to make my way back. As I passed a house with a giant blow-up pumpkin in the yard, I was jostled by a person in a mask and long flowing cloak. I turned to apologize for bumping into him but he grabbed hold of my arm. "Back off, or you and your friend will be very sorry." A ghoulish face with black holes for eyes stared at me as he pinched my arm tighter. Heart racing, I yelled for help but only a squeak came out. I brought up my arm with the umbrella to pommel him, but he knocked it away. Yanking my arm, I strove to shake him off. He held me a moment longer, then loosened his grasp and strode away.

I stood still a moment, stunned, my heart hammering in my chest. People swirling around me, seemed unaware of the danger I'd been in.

On shaky legs, I hurried to the middle of the street where there were fewer people and looked in the direction he'd taken. I couldn't see him. I searched as I walked on, but he'd vanished into the night.

At Willow Avenue I hesitated. Had he gone down this deserted street? Was he waiting in the bushes, ready to spring out at me? I dawdled for a few minutes, reached into a small reserve of gumption and started down the street.

I walked quickly, propelled by fear. Wind-driven leaves danced around my feet, and the rain pelted my umbrella. *He wouldn't give me a warning if he was planning to do me in, would he?* I kept to the middle of the road, away from shrubbery and trees, ready to run if he popped out at me. At last I reached Lake Street and joined a group of tots, moms, and dads strolling along. By the time I saw Ginger's house, my heart had stopped racing. Her porch light was a welcome beacon in the night. I waited at the bottom of her porch stairs until a cowboy and a witch snagged their booty and clambered down to the sidewalk.

"How was it?" Ginger asked with a grin.

"Amazing," I said. There was no need to scare her and put a damper on her fun.

The next little boy who came had hair slicked back from the rain and droplets streaming from his chin. After that came a girl of nine or ten-years, dressed in a flapper dress with no coat on.

"Aren't you cold?" Ginger asked.

"I'm f-f-freezing." She said, teeth chattering.

Due to the lateness of the night and her condition, she received a triple share of candy.

The last goblin and yeti left, and Ginger turned off her porch light. Moving into her living room, we warmed ourselves by the fire crackling in her woodstove. We'd given out candy to over two-hundred kids, including a few that were taller and more well-endowed than I. Other than the scary episode on Mitchell Street, it had been a wonderful night.

After some pleasant conversation, I noticed Ginger, the-rise-before-dawn-woman, fading fast. It was time to go. The only problem was my reticence to venture out into the darkness, where I might encounter the masked man. *Then again, I couldn't live inside forever, afraid to go out at night, could I?*

I left Ginger's friendly hearth and walked quickly to the car, my head swiveling in order to spot any sneak assailants. Opening the driver's side door, I checked the back seat and hatch-back area to make sure no one was lurking there in attack mode. All was safe. I got in, locked the doors and made an uneventful trip back to my house.

On my front porch I'd left a kettle full of candy with a sign for any stray trick-or-treaters to help themselves. The contents were about half gone. I unlocked my door, picked up the kettle and entered the house. Dashiell gave a joyful yip and ran to greet me. Marti was out with Frank tonight and probably wouldn't get back any time soon.

As Dash and I went for his last walk of the night, a disturbing thought crossed my mind. The masked man must know where I live and followed me to Ginger's house. Otherwise, how would he have found me in that crowd?

Chapter Thirty-Six

All Saints Day dawned clear and cold. This day is also called The Day of the Dead, but the name All Saints Day was more benign and to my liking. Dash and I were out and on our way to the county park by 7:30 in the morning. We meandered along as the sun crept higher above the horizon. The campground was closed for the season, and an air of desertion and loneliness hung over the entire park. At the northern end of the RV area, we walked along a wooded trail that would eventually lead to tent camping grounds.

As I shuffled through the multi-colored leaves, Dash darted ahead, chasing squirrels and exploring the smells and sounds of the hills beside the trail. I was deep into a reverie regarding Marti and Frank when a strong sensation of being watched washed over me. My errant mind careened back to the present as adrenaline shot through me. Swinging my head to the right, I caught a glimpse of color through the trees. Halting, I searched the forest, but all was still.

Where was Dash when I needed him? He'd let me know if there really was danger or if I was just imagining it. I padded quietly along, straining to hear any noises. Lots of people hiked this trail but next to none did on November First at 7:45 a.m. Snapping twigs sent my heart fluttering, but it was probably small woodland creatures going about their day's activities. At least I hoped so.

Suddenly I saw a flash of movement on the trail around an upcoming curve. I stopped, and around the bend bounded Dash. He skidded to a stop and sat in the path in front of me, a hopeful expression in his eyes. I dug in my pocket for a treat and held it out to him. He took it with his lips in his usual gentle manner. I attached his leash and turned around to retrace my steps. Two scares in as many days was too much for me. Dash and I moved out at a brisk pace and we were soon home.

Marti was still asleep so I pulled out our notes on the case and began to review them. We'd had Mandy and Sharon Pembower as well as Gerald's girlfriend, Mary, on our suspect list. Since it was definitely a man who had threatened me last night, I crossed them all off now. Of course, one of them could've sent someone else to do her dirty work, but it seemed unlikely. My money was still on Junior as the killer.

If only we could figure out a risk-free way to trap him.

"Is there any coffee?" Marti called out from the living room.

"Um, no. I'll put a pot on."

"Thanks." Marti left to get dressed. A few minutes later she appeared at my elbow and perused the paper in front of me. "You crossed off three names?"

"Yup. I'm pretty sure our perp is male."

She yawned and strolled over to the coffee maker. After pouring a cup she came back and sat across from me. "How come?"

I filled her in on my recent adventures.

"That's scary. Have you any idea who he was?"

"Nope. I can't even tell you for sure how tall he was, though he was bigger than I." Hmmn, Junior is kind of short. He may not be tall enough to be the man in the cloak.

Hot Dog

Marti looked thoughtfully out the window at my backyard. She turned her gaze on me. "Maybe we should take his advice. You know, back off."

"In some ways that makes sense. But, unfortunately, he knows who I am. Actually, he might know who you are, too."

She cradled her mug with both hands. "I see what you mean. Do you think we should tell Costas or Mitch about this?"

"I'd rather not. I don't think it'll do any good, and we'll probably just get a lecture about sticking our noses into police business." I hadn't told Marti about running into Mitch at Johnnie's. She was so happy to be back with Frank and I didn't want to throw cold water on that by whining about my relationship woes. Besides, I'd enjoyed spending time with Mitch, but it hadn't gotten very far, and no hearts were damaged. Marti interrupted my thoughts.

"What are we going to do?"

"First of all, be very careful. Secondly, I think we need to try to find out who this maniac is before he kills one of us."

"Do you have a plan to capture this guy?"

"No, I was trying to come up with something when you woke up."

"It would sure help in laying a trap if we knew who he was." She thought a moment and then brightened. "You just struck three people off the list, so we've definitely got cause to celebrate."

"Right. The only other thing we know for sure is that someone we talked with is probably the killer and is worried that we're closing in on him."

"We've talked to a lot of people."

"We have. Now I think our plan of action is to go back and talk to all of them again. Hopefully, we can figure out who he is before he strikes again."

Marti frowned. "I'd rather be in a little more control of my destiny."

I allowed myself a bit of the superior smirk of an experienced p.i. to briefly grace my visage. "Based on what I've seen of these cases, it doesn't work that way. You have to put yourself out there in order to connect the dots and solve the puzzle. But you're an engaged woman now and have a bright future ahead of you. If you want to pull out, I'll understand."

"What will you do as I'm 'pulling out' and running headlong into wedded bliss?"

Hot Dog

"I'll be forging ahead with all of the muscle and sinew within me to ferret out this monster, and bring him to justice. Meanwhile, you should have no cause for concern for my well-being. I'm certain I'll prevail, but if something, God forbid, should happen to me, at least I have no dependents."

"Oh, no? What about the Dasher?"

"I'm confident that one of my dog-walking friends would open up his or her home and heart to a beautiful dog such as Dash."

"As you know perfectly well, we're both in this up to our eyebrows. There will be no backing out for either one of us," Marti said. "All I meant by that destiny remark was that we should be able to come up with a plan that won't put our necks in jeopardy."

We discussed various options and came up with a few ideas but no grand scheme. I had work to do, so we decided to shelve our sleuthing until later in the day when we'd go back to visit Sharon Pembower. Since she was at the core of the matter, it seemed like the best place to start.

That afternoon, Marti came with me when I took Dash for his walk. *Just let some evildoer try to get the drop on me with Muscles Gonzalez by my side.*

We ran into Susan and Riley at the beach. We hadn't seen them for a while, so we caught up on each other's lives. Even though Dash was about twice as much dog as Riley, they rolled around and wrestled with each other as we walked along. We filled Susan in on our activities re: the Pembower Affair and asked her opinion.

She thought for a few minutes. "I'd be careful if I were you. It's getting really scary." She paused. "Doesn't it strike you that Junior didn't fall far from his daddy's tree?"

"That's for sure. My foot is still bruised from where that clod stomped on it," Marti said.

"I wouldn't put it past him to threaten someone, either, like that guy did to me," I said. "But I'm wondering now if he's the right guy. He might not be tall enough to be the man who threatened me on Halloween."

Susan frowned. "We'll all breathe a lot easier when this guy is caught. I—oh no. I think our time is up." She gave us a rueful grin. Riley, who had been bounding down the beach beside Dash, skidded to a stop and turned back toward us. As he ran by, he caught Susan's eye.

I saw that Marti looked as puzzled as I was.

"What's going on?" she said.

Susan rolled her eyes. "It's two-forty-five. He wants to be sure we get back in time for his favorite show. It starts at three."

Marti looked skeptical. "You mean he can tell time?"

Susan nodded. "I'll bet Dash knows when it's time for his dinner, doesn't he?"

"Yup, he does. He'll come into the kitchen and push his bowl around with his nose if I'm a minute late in serving it to him. I take it Riley's still hooked on the boob tube?" I asked.

She shook her head. "I think it's actually gotten worse. I'm seriously thinking about getting rid of my TV. That might be the only thing that will work. Anyway, great seeing you again." She turned and hurried after her addicted dog.

Chapter Thirty-Seven

After our walk, we drove over to see Sharon
Pembower at the dry cleaner's. Once again,
keen on killing two snakes with one stone,
I planned to pick up the clothes I had left
there several weeks ago. Instead of Sharon,
a woman in her twenties was at the counter.
We struck up idle chitchat with her as she
located my clothes and I paid for them.
From her we learned that it was Sharon's
day off.

Back in the car, I turned to Marti.
"This might actually work in our favor.
Monty probably won't have gone into work
his night shift yet."

"Unless they happen to be the killers,
in which case, with two of them there,
we'll be toast."

"You've never struck me as a glass-
half-emptiest individual."

"That's because I'm not. I'm merely
the voice of reason."

I had been driving as we conversed,
and I turned into the parking lot for their
apartment complex. "Can you honestly

picture either of those people as a killer?"

"All the evidence points to the fact that this was a crime done in the heat of the moment. I think that given the right circumstances, most of us could be guilty of murder. Therefore, even seemingly mild-mannered people such as Sharon and Monty could be killers. What we know of Pembower's abusive nature, it's not too much of a stretch for either Sharon or Monty to have gotten pushed over the edge."

"Yeah, you're right, but would they add to their body count by killing off two friendly amateur sleuths?"

She shrugged her shoulders. "I guess it depends on how desperate they are and how much of a threat they think we are."

"Got your cell phone in case we need it?"

"Yup." She hopped out of the car.

"Then I guess we'll soon see." Taking one of the small boxes stacked on the back seat, I hurried after her.

Knocking on Sharon's door, we heard some muffled conversation before the door opened. A small frown creased her face as recognition lit her eyes.

Connie Doherty

I gave her a warm smile. "Hi, Sharon. Sorry to bother you again, but we wanted to thank you and your husband for helping us with our case." I opened up the box and held it out to her. "I hope you like chocolate and peanut butter."

She smiled. "That's so nice of you. Won't you come in?" She stepped back and opened the door wider. "Look, Monty, what the girls brought us. You're going to love it."

I guess our plan to sweeten our way along with our peanut butter cups was paying off. We stepped into their living room. Monty, standing by the door to the kitchen, greeted us and walked over to his wife. He started to reach for a chocolate but Sharon snatched them away, laughing.

"You'll spoil your dinner."

"Please? Just one?"

"Oh, all right," she smiled.

He tasted part of one. "Wow. That's great. You made those?"

"She did." Marti said pointing to me.

"Sharon, you've got to get the recipe for them."

"I'd be happy to give it to you. They're easy to make. I'll drop it off for

you. Anyway, we can't stay, we don't want
to wear out our welcome."

"Nonsense. Have a seat," Monty said.

We sat in our usual places on their
sofa. Once everyone was settled, I looked
up. "How was your Halloween?" I asked.

Sharon smiled. "It was quiet. I worked
during the day, and Monty worked his
afternoon shift. We don't get many trick-
or-treaters here but Mandy brought my
grandson over." She smiled again. "He was
so cute. He went as a carrot."

Marti and I looked at each other.
Monty worked on Halloween. Deciding to take
a chance, I told them about my Halloween
threat. By the time I'd finished, both
Sharon and Monty were upset.

"This sounds very dangerous. Have you
thought of going to the police?" Monty
asked.

"I have, but I don't think they'd take
me seriously. Besides, I can't identify the
man." I looked directly at Sharon. "I hate
to ask this, but do you think that Junior
could be behind this?"

She looked quickly away as Monty
watched her closely. He got out of his
chair, walked over to stand behind her and
rested his hands lightly on her shoulders.

With his eyes on me, he said quietly, "Do you have good reason to suspect Gerry?"

"There's the matter of the inheritance," I said. "Did you know that Gerald was planning to change his will and leave all his money to the Henry Men?"

Monty looked thoughtful. "That was his militia group?"

"Yes."

"Whew, that does give him a pretty strong motive." He thought for another minute. "Sharon, call Junior and talk to him. Find out what he did on Halloween."

Sharon sat, still as a stone, looking away.

After a few moments, Monty said, "Shar, honey. Come on. We've got to help these ladies out. They're in danger. We all . . . we all need to know the truth . . . once and for all."

Sharon's shoulders had started shaking as she cried and covered her face with her hands.

Monty moved around to the front of the chair, squatted and embraced Sharon. "Come on, sweetie. You've got to do this."

"I know." Sharon stood. Composing herself, she wiped her eyes with a tissue and walked over to the phone. Bringing it

over by us she punched in some numbers.
After a few moments she said, "Hi Ger. How
are you? . . . I haven't talked with you in
a while. I got to thinking of you on
Halloween. I remembered how cute you looked
when you went as a clown that one year. Do
you remember that?" She paused, listening.
"Probably because I miss you. I don't see
you that often anymore. Did you have a nice
Halloween? . . . Oh, you had to work that
night? That's too bad, you used to love it
so . . ."

They talked a little longer, but we
could all see the relief in Sharon's eyes.
Marti and I could strike another name off
the list. Who was left?

Chapter Thirty-Eight

"Okay, we've got time for one more stop before dinner. Where do you want to go?" I said as we pulled out of the parking lot.

"Let's drop off a box of chocolates to Pete's friend, Zack."

"Great idea. We're even on the right side of town."

A few minutes later we were parked in front of Zack's place. The same blue Ford pickup truck was in the driveway. Just as before, after a couple of knocks we heard a dog barking and soon after, Zack opened the door.

"Hi. You missed Pete again."

"That's okay. We actually came to see you."

"In that case, come on in."

We followed him in and sat on his couch. "I hope you like chocolate."

Zack grinned. "Love it."

"How do you feel about peanut butter?"

"Even better, and especially when they're combined."

Hot Dog

"Two correct answers to our survey entitles you to one free box of peanut butter bars," I said and handed him the candy.

"Yum," he said, opening the box. He bit into one of the squares, closed his eyes and moaned. "These are great. Thanks."

We talked for a while about the dog, Marcie that he was still fostering. He said she needed lots of patience and love to turn her back into the kindhearted dog he knew was inside of her.

"Will you be able to adopt her out at some point?" Marti asked.

"That's the plan. There are always lots more dogs that need rescuing. I can't keep them all, so I need to get them to the point they'll be good family pets."

"Do they all turn around for you?"

Zack slowly shook his head as his face clouded over. "No, some of them had it too rough, or they just can't find it within themselves to forgive the human race for what was done to them."

"What happens to those poor guys?"

"Usually we can find a farm for them to live on, away from most people. Sometimes we have to send them to animal sanctuaries or put them down."

"That's terrible."

"It breaks your heart," he said
frowning.

"Do you do this for your job?" Marti
asked.

"No, I'm an industrial engineer."

"That's right. All of you guys have
day jobs. That's why I was the one who
looked after Roy."

He nodded. "Yeah, but also the police
were watching all of us."

I leaned forward. "Can I ask you
something, strictly on the q.t.? How do you
normally wind up with these dogs?"

"They come to us in lots of different
ways. The word is out there that we take in
Rotts, German shepherds, Pits and Pit-mixes
so people drop them off here at the house."

"Do you ever sort of liberate them if
they're being mistreated?"

"That would be breaking the law, now,
wouldn't it?" Zack said, looking me
straight in the eyes.

"Do you need to take the Fifth
Amendment?"

He smiled. "It might be a good time to
do that."

I smiled back. "Since we're in tough question mode, do you know what Pete was doing on Halloween night?"

Pete thought a moment. "He was going somewhere with Lacey. I think they went to one of the bars downtown. Do you need me to find out which one?"

"Um, it might help."

"Did they go out in costumes?" Marti asked.

Pete nodded, "I remember them talking about renting costumes from that Halloween store over by Meijers."

"Do you know how Pete was dressed?"

"Nope, I didn't see him that night. Why do you want to know?"

I related the story of my Halloween encounter.

He looked down at the floor for a moment then in a quiet voice asked, "And you think it might have been Pete?"

"I don't know. I hope not."

"I'll try to find out what he was wearing and call you when I have something."

"That would be great. Thanks."

We said our goodbyes and drove off, passing Pete on the road. We exchanged a wave.

"On, I'm starved," Marti said as we drove towards my house. "Why don't we save time and go out to dinner. My treat."

We decided on Johnnie's and arrived there ten minutes later. I was doubtful that a country and western bar would cater to vegetarians, but I can always find something to nibble on. Mary waved at us from the bar as we walked in, just like old times. She hurried over and gave us menus. Ten or so other diners were seated in various groups around the restaurant.

"Just so you know, there's no live entertainment tonight."

"That's fine. We've come for dinner."

Marti chose a hamburger and onion rings. I opted for salad and a baked potato, and we both decided on ice water. After Mary put our order in, she came back and talked with us.

"Did you enjoy the band the other night, hon?" She asked me.

"I did. They were easy to dance to."

"But you left before Jimmy did?" She asked, her eyebrows arched.

Hmmm, I wonder if she's interested in him again, now that Gerald is gone. "I get up about six and go to bed early. Besides, that wasn't a date, Jimmy and I are just friends. I didn't, um, step into your territory did I?"

"No. We had our little fling and that's that. He was real sweet when Ger died, though. He was right by my side the whole time." She shook her head and brushed at her eyes. "I really don't know what I would have done without him . . ." She was distracted by the bartender motioning to her. "I have to go. I have an order up." She scurried away.

We watched her take plates of food to a nearby table.

Mary made the rounds of the other tables picking up a few empty bottles before heading back to the bar for more beer. She swung back around to our table with two cold Buds. "Compliments of the man at the bar," she said and pointed.

Jimmy saluted as we spotted him.

Mary leaned in close and lowered her voice, "He wants to know if he can join you."

Marti and I exchanged a glance. "Sure," I said.

Mary waved him over. After he was seated and we exchanged our hellos, Mary said, "Jimmy, I haven't seen you since Halloween. You were lookin' fine out there on the dance floor with that cape swirling around you."

I heard blood rushing in my ears and jerked my head around to look at Marti. Regaining my composure, I saw Jimmy watching me, and quickly cut my eyes away.

Mary took Jimmy's order. Looking over her shoulder, she said, "I think your food is ready."

Marti and Jimmy made small talk as I sat in a daze. A few minutes later, Mary arrived with our food. "Thanks for the beer. Have an onion ring," Marti said, smiling and pushing her plate towards him.

He held his hand up, palm towards us, "No, you girls enjoy your dinner. Mine should be here in no time."

Somehow, I came up with the words to thank him as well and spread the dressing around my salad. We hadn't gotten too far along with our meals before Jimmy's burger and fries came.

"You're becoming quite the regulars here," Jimmy spread mustard and catsup on his bun.

Striving for normalcy, I smiled. "We had a late day and the cupboards were bare, so we decided to check out the food here.

How about you? You must come here a lot. You're here every time we are."

Jimmy finished chewing. "Yup, I am a regular. Don't like to cook and after a hard day's work, nothin's better than to sit down, eat, and pound back a couple of beers. Food's great isn't it?"

"Yeah, these rings are delicious," Marti said.

Jimmy looked over at my plate and frowned. "You not hungry?"

I smiled at him. "I'm a vegetarian."

His jaw dropped. "No."

I nodded. "For many years now."

"Well there's no time like the present. You eat a Johnnie-burger and you'll swear off those silly notions for good." He raised his hand to signal Mary.

She was leaning on the bar looking our way and came right over. "Mary, bring a burger for Onalee, here."

I shook my head. "No, please don't, Mary. I'm vegetarian and planning to stay that way."

Mary looked back and forth between us then directly at him. Her hands clenched at her hips. "Now, Jimmy, you heard her, she doesn't want a burger. She's got a

perfectly good dinner in front of her. Let
her be."

Jimmy grinned and threw up his hands.
"You womenfolk always stick together. I
know when I'm outnumbered."

With the crisis averted, we went back
to eating and listening to Jimmy talk about
his plans for the upcoming deer hunting
season.

When she saw we were finished with our
meals, Mary brought the checks over.
"Jimmy, shall I meet you out at the Rain
Bow, or are you picking me up?"

An angry look flashed in Jimmy's eyes,
but he quickly covered it with a smile.
"I'll pick you up."

"Doing some target practice?" I asked.

"Yup. I told you I thought girls with
guns was sexy," he said grinning. "You two
wanna join us?"

"What time?" Marti asked.

"We'd planned to go about 2:00," Mary
said. "It would be fun if you two came."

Marti and I looked at each other.
"Maybe we will." I had taken a few classes
at the Rain Bow and found I really enjoyed
it. "We'll meet you there if we can.
Thanks."

Hot Dog

"Lots of people wear capes on Halloween," Marti said as we drove back to my house.

"I know, but did you see the way he looked at me?"

"No, but he's always given me the creeps."

Chapter Thirty-Nine

Early the next morning, Marti arose to walk Dash with me. "I don't want you venturing out by yourself anymore. At least not until we have the perp behind bars."

It was a cold morning, and frost glistened on the rooftops around the neighborhood. Marti borrowed mittens, a neck gator and hat from me. As we made our way down to the beach, we saw familiar figures up ahead: Lacey and Kitty. Dash spotted them and bounded ahead to catch up to his friend.

Lacey waited for us but wasn't her usual ebullient self. After our hellos, she said, "Zack wanted to know what Pete was doing on Halloween. He was with me and we went to Mitchell's. Why does everyone want to know what we were doing?"

I really liked Lacey and didn't care to play fast and loose with the truth with her, but I was sure that her first allegiance was to Pete. She glared at me as I stalled. "Someone dressed in a cape threatened me on Halloween."

Hot Dog

"You still think it could've been Pete or maybe even Pete and I who killed Pembower, don't you? You call yourself a friend, but you don't trust me." She turned and stormed away down the beach.

Marti and I looked at each other. I shrugged and we started after her. We walked behind her for about ten minutes, and heard her call Kitty to come. The dog raced up to her. She attached her leash and turned to retrace her steps. When she got close to us, she said, "I'm heading back because I have to be in to work early today. Nice seeing you." With blazing eyes, she and Kitty strode away.

Dash had followed Kitty but now stayed with us, watching her. Kitty turned her head once to look at us but then turned back.

"That was uncomfortable," Marti said.

"Sure was. I wonder if other amateur sleuths wind up losing friends left and right."

"If they do, it's certainly not brought out in the chronicles, is it?"

"Nope. If some of the bad parts were given more coverage, maybe every Thomasina, Dick and Harriet wouldn't be pining away to fill the gumshoes of the amateur sleuth."

Connie Doherty

As we were engrossed in our conversation, Dash took to his heels and ran up the nearest dune. He galloped along the dune tops and turned to enter the wooded area behind them.

"I don't like him getting so far away from us. You never know what he's going to get into," I said. We scrambled into the dunes and tried to spot him. He was nowhere.

"Maybe we can follow his trail, On."

It soon became apparent that tracking wasn't in our skill set. We kept to the ridge-line of the hills thinking we could catch a glimpse of him. We got to about where I'd lost sight of him. "Let's climb down and see if he's anywhere in these woods," I said. We continued calling him. He was pretty good about coming when I wanted him to, unless he was distracted by an exciting smell. We searched the forest and kept yelling his name. We went as far as the tent campground with no dog in sight. Searching the area, we saw nothing but a couple of squirrels. Back out on the beach, we could see several miles in both directions. There was no darting black spot midst the golden sand.

Hot Dog

Nearly a half-hour had elapsed since last I'd seen him, and I was very upset. He'd never disappeared from me this long.

"We'll find him, On. Don't worry."

"Let's head back along the trail for a while. He loves going that way because so many dogs pass through there."

"Good idea."

Taking one last look up and down the beach, we went back through the campground to the trailhead. Walking along, we stopped periodically to search the woods on both sides of us, Marti and I calling for my lost boy. The trail wound around, making abrupt turns. It was probably cut that way to save as many trees as possible.

Coming around a sharp turn, we nearly ran into Tommy, hiding behind a tree. A chill ran through me right to my toes, and both Marti and I halted.

We all stared at each other for a moment. Finding my voice I said, "Tommy, I've lost my dog. Have you seen him?"

"Yup."

"Today?"

"Yup."

"Where?" I might have screamed the word because he took a step back and eyed me. "Please. I'm really worried about him."

"He was with some guy over thataway,"
he said and pointed to his left, further
into the woods. "I thought it was funny
that your dawg was with the other feller."
      "When was this?"
      "A few minutes ago."
      "Which direction were they headed?"
Marti asked.
      "Towards the highway."
      I started off headlong into the
undergrowth, Marti behind me.
      "Wait!" Tommy screamed at us. We
stopped and turned back towards him. "He's
got a gun."
      "No," I yelled and started running
again. I was sobbing. My beautiful dog in
the hands of a maniac with a gun.
      "On, I'm calling 9-1-1. We should wait
for them!" Marti yelled.
      I misjudged the width of a fallen limb
and fell over it.
      "Are you okay?" Marti asked, reaching
where I lay.
      "I'm fine," I said, huffing, and
clambered to my feet. I heard a sharp bark.
It was Dashiell. It had to be. I starting
running again. Marti caught up and pulled
my arm.

Hot Dog

"Stop! This is a trap. We've got to slow down."

I heard a dog cry out in pain. I tore off again. Marti was right, but I now knew what it meant to see red. I was furious. Someone was hurting my beloved Dashiell. I burst through pine trees at the top of a small hill. There was Dash, tied to a tree on the other side of a small clearing. He saw me and lunged, barking a greeting, but a rope stopped him. I scrambled to get to him.

"Halt," thundered a voice to my right. There stood Jimmy, legs akimbo training a gun on me.

I skidded to a stop, my heart pounding. I needed to think. All of our lives depended on it. "Hi, Jimmy. I'm glad it's you who found my dog. I'm just going to untie him and take him home."

"Can't let you do that," he shook his head. "You just had to pretend to be a girl detective, didn't you? Couldn't leave well enough alone."

"Why'd you do it? You and Ger were best friends."

He nodded. "Yup, and I miss him every day," he sighed. "Guess I always will."

"It was an accident, I'll bet."

"I guess you could say that. I tried to reason with him. He took my Mary away from me and I love her."

"You'd had a few beers before you went over to his house."

Again he nodded. "Ger was all worked up over his dog and those good for nothin' bleeding heart animal rights wackos he'd fought with." He looked up at me sorrowfully. "You know if he hadn't gotten into it with them just before I happened by, maybe things would've been different."

"Have you got a good shot—" *Oops, terrible word choice.* "With Mary now?"

"Yup, I think I do. But then you two girls come around and muddy up the works."

We needed to keep on the topic of Jimmy and Mary, and give the police time to get here. "Jimmy, Mary talked about how good you were when she was grief-stricken. How you stayed right by her side. You were a good friend to her."

"Thank you, ma'am. I put a big store on friendship."

"I know you do. I'm glad to have you as a friend."

His eyes narrowed. "Speaking of friends. Where's the other girlie?"

"I have no idea."

Hot Dog

"Don't get cute with me. You two was together earlier. Call her. Now!" He barked. His gun which he'd lowered was aimed at my chest again.

"Okay. Marti!" I paused. "Marti, come over here!"

We waited, but she didn't come. Jimmy's head was cocked, trying to hear her. I listened as hard as he did, but for the sweet sounds of sirens coming to our rescue.

"If she don't show herself by the time I count to ten, I'm going to have to put a bullet through your heart."

"Jimmy, you don't want any more killing. We called 9-1-1. The police will be here soon. From what you said, you would probably only be charged with manslaughter. Things just got out of hand. You didn't mean to shoot Ger, but two more killings would put you in prison for the rest of your life."

"Get her over here." He commanded.

I called again for Marti and repeated what Jimmy said. All this time Dash watched intently, mostly keeping his eyes on me.

"One . . . two . . . three . . . four," Jimmy counted then stopped to listen. I heard twigs snapping behind me as Marti emerged.

"Jimmy, the police know you killed Pembower. I have 9-1-1 on the line right now. Want to talk with them?" She held her phone out to him.

He swung his gun around to her. Still no sirens. How could they find us in time, here in the deep woods?

Suddenly, out of the corner of my eye, I saw something fly through the air. A thick branch slammed into Jimmy's head and he reeled backwards. Dash growled and lunged at the rope. Marti and I both ran over to Jimmy. He was knocked unconscious. Marti picked up the gun and stepped away from him, keeping him in sight. I bounded over to Dash and released him. He was fine. I started to hug him, but he broke free of me. Bolting to Jimmy, he stood over him, growling.

I looked in the direction the flying stick had come from. Tommy stood in the trees. As our eyes met, he lifted his hand and saluted before turning and slinking away.

Epilogue

Three weeks later-just to wrap things up:

1. Jailhouse Jimmy is awaiting trial without bail. Of course he's innocent until proven guilty, but the gumshoes of GOO (Gonzalez-O'Conner Operatives) are convinced that he'll soon be doing a stretch in the big house.

2. Ginger held her soup-er-cookie bake-off and garnered enough money to keep about seventy little kids warm this winter.

3. I entered with my peanut butter bars and a soup but didn't place in either category.

4. Lacey entered with an original recipe for sauerkraut ginger snaps. Two judges went home sick. The cooking lessons have recommenced.

5. Marti and Frank are billing and cooing though Ms. Gonzalez has returned to Metro Detroit.

6. Roy was adopted by a single woman from Saginaw who loves him and takes him to the dog park nearly every day.

7. Pete and Lacey are also twosoming it. Lacey is secretly hoping to get a ring for Christmas.

8. As for me, Mitch and I haven't crossed paths again as of the time of this writing. As I always say, lucky in dogs, unlucky in love. I received a grudging acknowledgement of my help in the case from Mr. Costas. Although, he maintained that they knew Jimmy was the murderer and were in the process of gathering enough evidence to convict him.

As soon as the weather breaks, I plan to put the ficus at the curb for any passerby foolish enough to want it. Meanwhile, Dash and I are having a rollicking good time in our first heavy snowfall.

Recipes

I didn't enter this soup or the following peanut butter bar recipe in the cook-off but I should have.

Nick's Thick as Fog Pea Soup

1 Bag of split peas
2 stalks of celery
2 medium carrots
1 large onion
3-5 medium potatoes
4-5 smoked pork chops (meat eaters' version)
Liquid smoke to taste (vegetarian version)
Salt and pepper to taste

Rinse the peas and check for foreign matter. Cover the peas with water in a soup pot. Bring to a boil. Turn off the heat and set aside for one hour. Meanwhile, prepare the other ingredients as follows: Thinly slice the onion, cube the pork chops, cube the potatoes, use a peeler to shave thin slices from the carrots and celery. After the peas are softened, dump the rest of the ingredients (except the liquid smoke if using) into the soup pot and bring to a boil. Simmer for two to four hours until thickened. It can be further thickened with instant mashed potatoes. Vegetarians- the liquid smoke should be added at the end.

Killer Peanut Butter Bars

Bars
2 Cups peanut butter
1/2 Cup melted butter
1 box (4 1/2 cups) powdered sugar
3/4 cup brown sugar
1/2 teaspoon vanilla

Topping
2 Cups chocolate chips
2 tablespoons butter

Mix the bar ingredients (The first five), well. Put on a lightly greased cookie sheet. Roll out or pat-in to a thickness of 1/4 inch.

Melt the chocolate chips and two tablespoons of butter in the microwave, following the directions for melting the chips on the package. Spread the chips mixture thinly across the top of the bars. Cut them into squares immediately. Refrigerate.